Northern Star

Lorna Schultz Nicholson

James Lorimer & Company Ltd., Publishers
Toronto

James Lorimer & Company Ltd. acknowledges the support of the Ontario Arts Council. We acknowledge the support of the Government of Canada through the Book Publishing Industry Development Program (BPIDP) for our publishing activities. We acknowledge the support of the Canada Council for the Arts for our publishing program. We acknowledge the support of the Government of Ontario through the Ontario Media Development Corporation's Ontario Book Initiative.

Cover illustration: Greg Ruhl

The Canada Council | Le Conseil des Arts
for the Arts | du Canada

ONTARIO ARTS COUNCIL
CONSEIL DES ARTS DE L'ONTARIO

Library and Archives Canada Cataloguing in Publication
Schultz Nicholson, Lorna

Northern star / by Lorna Schultz Nicholson.

ISBN10 1-55028-911-X (board); ISBN13 978-1-55028-911-4 (board)

ISBN10 1-55028910-1 (pbk.); ISBN13 978-1-55028-910-7 (pbk.)

  I. Title.
PS8637.C58N67 2006   jC813'.6   C2006-901150-8

James Lorimer & Company Ltd.,
Publishers
317 Adelaide St. West
Suite 1002
Toronto, Ontario
M5V 1P9
www.lorimer.ca
Printed and bound in Canada.

Distributed in the United States by:
Orca Book Publishers
P.O. Box 468
Custer, WA USA
98240-0468

Contents

1	Tournament	9
2	Shootout	14
3	The Gazette	21
4	Dylan's Excitement	27
5	Lots of Goals	32
6	In Demand	40
7	Oilers Game	44
8	Cheap Shot	49
9	Peter in *The Sun*	54
10	Signing Autographs	62
11	City Girls	68
12	Olds Fans	74
13	Steele vs. Kuiksak	80
14	Interested Agent	87
15	Peter's Dad	92
16	Trevor's Advice	97
17	More Ups and Downs	103
18	Actions Speak Louder Than Words	108

Acknowledgements

Once again, I must thank the Lorimer team. They take my draft and make fabulous suggestions to create a better book. I so appreciate the attention to detail that goes into publishing good books at James Lorimer and Co.

I want to thank Hockey Canada for all their support. Brad Pascall for putting my books on www.hockeycanada.ca, and Paul Carson for lending me coaching and drill manuals and answering any questions I ask.

I would also like to thank Jacquie Fredericks for using my books in the Read and Succeed program that she put together for the Pentiction Vees. And to Dale Saip, Ron Toigo and the Vancouver Giants for allowing me to share in their reading program as well. I feel fortunate that the hockey communities in Canada are embracing my books as part of their literacy programs.

Of course, my biggest thank you goes to you, my readers. I love your mail so keep it coming. Enjoy!

To Dorothy Nicholson,
a wonderful mother-in-law and friend

1

Tournament

Peter Kuiksak and Josh Watson stood by the tournament desk, reading the game charts. Josh playfully punched Peter's arm and said, "We play you in the gold medal game tomorrow. See? Arrows and Rockies."

"We just squeaked in," replied Peter, pointing to the red markings on the chart, "because Fort McMurray beat St. Albert in overtime. It went to a shootout!"

"I've only been in one shootout before," said Josh. "I had to take the last shot. It was really nerve-racking!"

"We're going to whup you," said Peter, grinning.

"Yeah, right," said Josh. "We've got Sam in net and he's the best goalie in the league. We haven't lost a game all tournament."

Peter smiled with attitude. "Don't forget, I know Sam's weakness."

* * *

In the Sherwood Park Arrows dressing room the next day, Peter got his gear on in record time. His stomach was tied up in knots. He snapped on his helmet, leaned against the wall and jiggled his leg. Greg sat on one side of him and Dylan on the other. Dylan turned to Peter and said, "You only need to get two points to be top scorer in the tournament."

Peter shrugged. "I don't care about that. I just want us to win."

"As if," said Greg, butting in the conversation. "You'll probably carry the puck on your own just so you can win the trophy."

Peter ignored Greg and didn't reply. Greg was always making snide comments about Peter. Usually Peter avoided sitting beside him in the dressing room, but today, he was too excited to care who he sat beside.

The door swung open and Coach John announced that the ice was ready. Peter sucked in a deep breath, exhaled, and stood up. Matt, the captain of the team, yelled out, "Who's going to win?"

All the guys chanted, "Arrows, Arrows."

Peter tried to chant along with the team, but he had a hard time making his voice as loud as the yells of the rest of the guys. On game day, he found it difficult to talk. All morning at the Patterson's he had barely said anything to anyone. He'd eaten breakfast, then gone upstairs to his room to stretch out on his bed, stare at the ceiling, and think of hockey plays.

* * *

Peter blasted onto the ice, skating at full speed, whipping around the corners. He heard the crowd and glanced at the packed stands. Quickly, he looked away. He couldn't waste energy thinking about the fans.

The warm-up flew by. After what seemed like just seconds the whistle blew to start the game. Peter skated toward the bench. Coach John had already prepped the Arrows in the dressing room and given out positions and lines. Peter was to take centre on the first line. He joined the circle at the bench and listened as Coach hyped them up.

"Make sure you play your own game," said Coach. "In the offensive zone, the first two fore-checkers go hard to the puck, and the third forward stays high." He made eye contact with every player before he continued. "Remember, they will try to break the guy up the middle. In your own end, don't be running around chasing the puck, play good defensive position. Wingers stay high on the point. Centres stay down low. And defence clear the front of the net. Now, what's the name of our team?"

"Arrows, Arrows!"

This time Peter barely managed a whisper.

Peter skated over to centre and positioned his hands on the stick for the face-off, just like Coach John had taught him. He put his left hand low and stared intently at the ref's hand. His hands were shaking. He wanted that puck.

As soon as the puck dropped, Peter slapped it back to his defence. Tanner, on left wing, skated ahead. On the other side, Greg also skated forward. Peter would have to stay high, as he was the third guy going in. Tanner skated wide, now carrying the puck. Peter kept pace and slowed down only when he was well over the blue line. He headed directly to the net. Tanner looked up, saw that Greg wasn't open, and looked for Peter. Peter hit the hash marks at full speed and tapped his stick. Tanner fired the puck to Peter, who one-timed it toward Sam's blocker. Peter knew that Sam was quick with his glove hand but his weakness was his blocker side.

The puck sailed into the top corner. The crowd cheered.

Tanner rushed over and jumped on Peter. Greg congratulated Peter too, but not in the same way. He just patted his back.

On the bench, Coach tapped Tanner on the helmet. "Great swivel head, Tanner. You found the open man." Then he patted Peter on the back. "Great shot. You timed it perfectly."

Peter beamed.

The score remained 1–0 for the rest of the first period. Peter had lots of chances to score, but Sam was technically sound and awesome with his glove hand. Also, it was near impossible to get a wrap-around in on him, as he totally covered the side of the net. When the buzzer sounded the end of the period, both teams filed into their dressing rooms. Peter sat down and unsnapped his helmet. He leaned against the wall and closed his eyes. They had to maintain their lead.

Coach came in and gave them the pep talk. He told them to keep playing the way they were and to shoot low at the goalie instead of high.

The puck dropped to start the period. On Peter's first shift, he managed to get one shot away, but that was all. The Calgary Rockies were strong defensively, clearing the puck the instant it was in front of their net.

Peter was out of breath when he headed in for a line change. He sat on the bench, put his head down, and closed his eyes. His heart raced and his chest moved up and down. Suddenly, he heard the crowd yelling and jumped up. The Rockies had a breakaway!

The Rockies forward slipped the puck through the legs of the Arrows defence, raced around him, faked the shot, then went to his backhand and roofed it. The puck zinged into the back of the net. Now the score was 1–1.

"Peter," yelled Coach. "Your line next. Greg, you sit. Matt, you go in for Greg."

Peter watched Greg slump onto the bench. Why was Coach shortening the bench already? They were only midway through the second period.

Peter dug in his edges and skated forward. He would go deep, as he was second man in. Tanner would have to stay high. Matt carried the puck too far and ended up in a battle along the boards. Peter skated in for support. He lined up the Rockies player who was tying up Matt and levelled him in a good clean hit. The boards shook. Matt capitalized on Peter's hit and picked up the loose puck. Peter sped to the back of the net so Matt could nail him with a pass. With the puck on his stick, Peter looked for Tanner. When he saw him trying to stay open out front, he fired the puck to him. Tanner took a low hard snap shot. The puck deflected out. Peter took a stride forward, stuck out his stick, and backhanded the puck.

Sam tried to block it with his shoulder but it bounced over and in. The Arrows were once again up by a goal!

Nearing the end of the third period, the score was still 2–1 for the Arrows. Peter had hardly been off the ice during this last period. Sweat dripped from his forehead. His legs ached.

With thirty seconds left, the Rockies pulled their goalie. Up by only one goal, the Arrows had to play good defence. The seconds ticked by. The play remained in the Arrows end. The crowd started counting down the last ten seconds. When they hit six, the puck was passed back to a Rockies defence. Peter tried to swat at it as it was passed over, but he couldn't reach it. The Rockies defence moved in.

Caught on his heels, the Arrows winger backed off. In that split second, the Rockies defence fired off the most amazing slapshot. Stu, the Arrows goalie, didn't have a chance.

The score was tied. The game would go into overtime.

2

Shootout

The score was still 2–2 after ten minutes of overtime. Tournament rules stated that, if there was still no winner after ten minutes of overtime, the game would go to a shootout. The Arrows players huddled around Coach at the boards. Coach had one knee on the bench.

"Greg, you'll go first, followed by Tanner, Matt, Peter, and Gage."

Peter sucked in a deep breath. He was glad he didn't have to go first.

After a meeting at centre ice with the two captains, the ref motioned for the Rockies to take the first shot. Peter watched the Rockies player line up. The guy took off and sped toward the goalie at full speed. When he ripped the puck toward the top corner, Stu flung his hand in the air for an unbelievable save. Peter pounded the boards in excitement.

Then Greg lined up at centre ice. At full speed, he approached Sam. He tried to deke him and toe-drag the puck in front. He almost had him, but Sam aggressively stick-checked the puck. His shoulders slumped, Greg skated toward the bench. This time it was the Rockies bench that went wild. Coach patted Greg on the head. "Good effort," he said.

Greg stood beside Matt on the bench. Peter was next to Matt, waiting his turn. "My father is going to be mad at me," Greg muttered to Matt. Peter overheard the comment, and couldn't imagine his own father being mad at him for missing a shot.

"Tell him that after the game you asked Coach to help you work on the shootout. That will make him happy," said Matt quickly, before he turned his head to stare at the ice, where the Rockies shooter was heading toward Stu. "Come on, Stu, you can do it," he said.

The guy shot right at Stu, who made an easy pad save. Peter banged his hand against the boards, then turned to Tanner. "Don't go for the glove on Sam — he's too good. Hit him on his blocker side."

Tanner nodded and skated to centre ice. When he took off, Peter sucked in a deep breath. *Come on, you can do it, Tanner.* Tanner faked right, then toe-dragged the puck, popping it in on the blocker side with a backhand. Peter threw his hands in the air! After two shooters each, the Arrows were winning the shootout 1–0.

The next Rockies player lined up at centre ice. He zipped down and tried for a five-hole shot, but Stu kept his legs together and the puck bounced off his pads.

Now it was Matt's turn. Matt nervously skated in a tight circle at centre ice, waiting for the whistle to blow. He started a couple of strides from the puck, taking a run at it. Peter whispered to Tanner, "Is it better to start fast?"

"Yeah," said Tanner. "You have to give it at the beginning."

Peter drew in a breath. His throat was dry.

Matt snapped the puck at Sam's five-hole. Sam made the save, but somehow lost his balance and fell back. The ref motioned that the puck was in, and Matt fell down to one knee and pumped his arm in a victory cheer. The crowd went nuts.

The Arrows bench went ballistic. Peter leaned over the bench. Matt skated to the bench and slapped everyone's hand.

Sam slammed his stick on the ice and skated out of the goalie crease. The Arrows were leading the shootout 2–0.

When the next Rockies shooter managed to deke around Stu and sink his shot in the right top corner, Peter's stomach churned. It was 2–1. Peter was the fourth shooter — if he put the puck in the net, the Arrows would win without Gage taking the last shot. If he missed, then there was a chance for the Rockies to tie it up. If that happened, Coach would have to pick five new guys for a new shootout.

Peter swigged down some water before he skated to centre ice. His skin felt clammy. His hands were slippery and soaking wet under his gloves. He stared at Sam down at the end of the rink, who was psyching himself by batting each post with his stick. Then Sam got into his crouch.

Peter moved away from the puck so he could get a good run at it. He heard the whistle blow and he skated three hard strides.

He had to make Sam go down.

Nearing to the net, Peter saw Sam deepen his crouch. Peter wound up for a slapshot. Sam anticipated and took a stride forward to cut down the angle. But Peter faked the shot and deked. Knowing he was duped, Sam immediately swooped over to try to punch the puck away from Peter. Peter held on to the puck, but barely. He caught it on the toe of his stick and flipped it up. Sam slid … but he just wasn't quick enough. The puck caught the side of his arm and bounced. The puck was in!

Immediately, Peter raised his arms in victory. The entire Arrows team jumped over the boards, throwing their gloves and helmets in the air. They raced over to Peter and knocked him flat on the ice.

It took five minutes to get the ice cleared of helmets and gloves. Then both teams lined up on the blue lines for the awards ceremony.

"The Most Valuable Player for today's game," said the announcer over the PA system, "is number 54 from the Sherwood Park Arrows, Peter Kuiksak."

Peter skated toward the trophy table. All the guys tapped their sticks on the ice. He shook hands, accepted his trophy, and returned to the blue line.

"And now for our tournament top scorer," the announcer's voice seemed to get louder with each word. "Number 54," the crowd erupted in cheers, "from the Sherwood Park Arrows, Peter Kuiksak!"

* * *

In the dressing room, Dylan talked non-stop to Peter about the awards. But Greg didn't say a word to him. Like Greg, Tanner was silent. Tanner and Matt were the best players on the Arrows, and Peter knew that either one could have easily been named MVP too. So Peter concentrated on getting dressed. He couldn't wait to phone home and tell his father and Susie what he won. They'd be happy for him.

Peter showered and headed out to the lobby. He wanted to catch Josh and Sam before they headed back to Calgary.

"I can't believe you won both MVP and top scorer," said Josh, trying to be upbeat. Even so, Peter could tell he was upset with the Rockies loss.

"I thought I had you," said Sam. His eyes looked red, as if he might have been crying. "I can't believe I missed your shot."

"Do you guys have another tournament coming up?" Peter wanted to change the subject.

Josh nodded. "During Christmas break, we're in Kelowna. What about you guys?"

"We're there too!" Out of the corner of his eye, Peter saw Christine waving at him.

"It's by far the best Bantam tournament in the west," said Josh. "All the best Bantam teams are... there." Josh slowly turned to see who Peter was looking at. When he turned back, he was grinning like crazy. "Who's *that*?"

"Christine Patterson. I billet at her house."

"You billet with *her*?" Josh glanced at Christine again. "She's hot! Is she in grade eight too?"

"No, grade nine," said Peter. "But we're in the same junior high." Peter knew all the guys on his team agreed with Josh about Christine. Peter didn't think she was that hot — more like kind of annoying — but he liked to play along with the guys. He knew she was one of the popular girls at school. Peter had sent a picture of her to his friends at home in Tuktoyaktuk to see their reaction.

"Excuse me," a low voice said from outside the circle.

All three boys turned. A dark-haired man, holding a spiral-bound notebook, stood beside Peter. He didn't look much older than some of the senior students at the high school.

"Are you Peter Kuiksak?" he asked.

"Ye-ah," replied Peter, taking a step back. The man stuck out his hand.

"My name is Spencer Mann and I'm the sports reporter for the Sherwood Park *Gazette*."

He tilted his head just a little. "Would you mind if I asked you a few questions?"

Did he say reporter? Peter didn't know how to answer the guy, so he stood ramrod straight, choking on any words that might possibly come out of his mouth.

Josh elbowed Peter in the ribs and whispered, "Go for it." His eyes were wide with excitement.

"Yeah, go for it," said Sam. He sounded excited too.

"I have just a few questions. It won't take long," said Spencer Mann. "I want to write a short piece on you for our sports section."

"Come on, Sam," said Josh. "Let's leave Peter alone. We have to go anyway." Josh patted Peter on the back. "E-mail me later, okay?" Then he grinned, leaned forward, and whispered in his ear, "You're going to be famous."

Peter watched Sam and Josh walk away before he turned to face the reporter.

"How does it feel to be named MVP and top scorer?" Spencer Mann clicked his pen and smiled at Peter.

"Good, I guess."

"Are you enjoying living in Edmonton?"

"Yeah," replied Peter.

"Do you miss home?"

"Sometimes."

Spencer Mann smiled as if he was trying to put Peter at ease. Peter knew his one-word answers were not giving the reporter much to work with, but he couldn't help himself.

"Can you tell me a little about home?" Spencer asked. "I know you have brothers and sisters. What do they think about you living in Edmonton?"

Finally, Peter felt as if he could say more than a word or two. Susie and his other siblings were a good topic. He told the reporter how his family was really supportive, and he mentioned Susie by name. If they printed her name, Peter could cut the article out and send it to her. She'd be thrilled. As Peter talked, the reporter wrote in some sort of weird cryptic handwriting.

When Peter stopped talking, the reporter looked up. "What was the hockey like up there?"

"Not very good. That's why I'm here."

"What do you think of the Sherwood Park coaches? Have they helped you improve?"

"Oh, yeah. I've learned tons. They're the best."

"What do you think of the guys on your team?"

"They're good guys."

"Last question," said Spencer Mann. "What is it that makes you such a good player? Is it raw talent? Desire? Competitive drive? I'll ask your coaches this question as well, but I'd like to get your answer first."

Peter hunched his shoulders and lowered his head. "I don't know." How was he supposed to answer this question? Finally, he looked up and said, "I like hockey, so I try hard."

Spencer shoved his pen in his notebook just as his cell phone rang. He held up his hand and said, "Thanks. I really appreciate your time." Then he answered his phone.

Peter picked up the handle of his bag and walked toward where Mr. Patterson was waiting.

3

The Gazette

"Who were you talking to at the arena?" Christine asked on the way home in the Patterson's van.

"Guys I went to hockey camp with," replied Peter. He sat in one of the captain seats and Christine the other. Andrew, Christine's younger brother, had the back seat to himself.

"I didn't mean them," she said. "I was talking about that other guy. The older dark-haired guy."

"You mean the newspaper reporter?"

"You were talking to a *reporter?*"

Peter turned to stare out the window.

"Is he, like, writing an article on you or something?"

From the back seat, Andrew piped up. "Did they take pictures of you with your trophies? When will it be in? What newspaper?"

"The Sherwood *Gazette*, I think." Peter slumped in his seat.

"Oh." Christine glanced out the window, suddenly bored with the conversation. "That's just a little paper. When you said 'newspaper,' I thought you meant the *Edmonton Sun*. The *Gazette* only comes out every Wednesday." Christine rolled her eyes. "My brother was always in that paper. It doesn't mean much."

Mr. Patterson looked in his rearview mirror. "Never mind, Christine. What kind of questions did he ask, Peter?"

"Just stuff about hockey and my family."

"How exciting for you," said Mrs. Patterson from the front seat. "You deserve some credit after the way you played during this tournament." She turned and smiled at him.

"Did you mention me?" Andrew bounced in the back seat.

"I can't really remember what I said," mumbled Peter.

"You better not have mentioned me," uttered Christine. "I'd be so embarrassed."

* * *

In his room at the Patterson's, Peter picked up the phone. He usually called home on the weekend and once during the week. He'd called home the day before, but he wanted to tell his family about the awards and the reporter. He quickly punched the string of numbers.

"Hey, Susie," he said, "Guess what! A reporter talked to me tonight and wants to do an article on me."

"Wow, Peter, you're making the big time."

"Not really. It's just a little paper. But I mentioned you." Peter played with the telephone cord.

"Me?! I'm going to be in a newspaper in Edmonton?"

He smiled just thinking of Susie's face breaking into a wide grin. "I hope so. I told him about you."

"You have to send me the article. I'll show all my friends."

"As soon as it's out, I'll send it to you for sure. Is Dad there? I want to talk to him too."

"Yeah, he just got in from a hunt. You should see the size of the caribou he got this time. The boys are skinning it now. I told Dad I want the fur to make a blanket for Baby Lisa. I need a blanket for her when we're at the arena. You know how cold it is in there. Hockey is going to start soon."

"Is it cold enough yet to get the ice going?" Peter asked. In Tuktoyaktuk, the arena ice was natural ice. In the North, they didn't use refrigeration units to make ice. None of the arenas were heated either, or else the ice would melt. Often Peter played hockey until his toes were numb.

"Pretty soon," said Susie. "We're going to miss you playing, though. You scored all the goals."

"I wish I could teach the guys up there the stuff I've learned here, about plays and skating techniques and even how to hold your hands to win a face-off. I bet Jason scores all the goals now."

"Yeah, probably. It's so good you're playing hockey in Edmonton but ..." Susie paused, then changed the subject. "You should see the size of the bones on this caribou. They'll be great for the boys. They're doing really beautiful carvings to sell."

"Maybe they'll make enough money to come see me. Are you making soup tonight?" Peter longed for Susie's caribou soup. She would make huge pots and the house would smell so good. There was no caribou meat at the Patterson's, only chicken and beef. Peter could almost taste the tender meat he loved so much. Sometimes he couldn't believe what he'd given up to play hockey, but it had all been worth it so far.

"It's already on the stove. A big, big pot. Today I put both rice and potatoes in. Here, I'll hold the phone near the pot so you can smell it," she teased him.

"You have to promise to make me some when I come home," said Peter, laughing.

"Are you going to be here at Christmas? You can't miss solstice."

"I don't know yet," said Peter. "We don't have our schedule."

"You have to come home. It won't be the same without you."

"I know. Listen, I need to talk to Dad."

"Okay. But think about what I said. I miss you." Peter heard her drop the phone and yell, "Dad!"

While Peter waited for his dad to pick up the phone, he thought about home. Talking to Susie made so many images flash in his mind — snowmobiling on the frozen Arctic Ocean, playing hockey in an arena so cold everyone's breath froze in front of their faces, walking to school in parkas and crowboots, eating muktuk after a whale had been harpooned. Things were so different there. Life was quieter, slower-paced, and way less complicated. Everyone knew everyone and there were no big malls or huge stores. You shopped for groceries at one store, which had everything in it from apples to screwdrivers. No one really bought meat at the store. Everybody hunted for meat. And out on a hunt, no one spoke, and there was time to think or just be quiet.

In Edmonton, life hurried along and there was no time for anything. The teachers at school gave so much homework, and kids were always running from place to place. And everywhere you went, you had to drive in a vehicle. The roads were busy and there were traffic jams. At home, in the winter, Peter drove a snowmobile everywhere, and a traffic jam consisted of three cars backed up.

"Hi, Peter. What's up?" His dad interrupted his thoughts.

"Hi, Dad." Peter felt a lump in his throat. He twisted the phone cord around his finger. "I won MVP and top scorer for the tournament."

"That's great, Pete. Good for you."

"And a reporter is writing an article on me too."

"A reporter? Really? That's something. I'm proud of you,

Pete. Keep up the good work. Listen, I can't talk long. We're skinning the caribou. You should see it, Pete. It's huge. The boys were with me on the hunt."

"Did they do good?"

"They were great."

"Okay, well, I'll let you go."

"Send the paper when the story on you comes out."

"Okay, Dad. Say hi to everyone for me."

Peter hung up the phone and immediately went to his closet. He pulled out the drum he'd brought with him when he'd moved from Tuk. Dust covered it. The teachers gave him so much homework that, with hockey everyday too, he hardly had time to play the drum. He sat on his bed, and was about to drum his fingers against the caribou hide when he heard a knock on his door.

"Hey, Peter," said Andrew. "You want to play mini-sticks?"

* * *

When Peter arrived at school on Wednesday morning, Dylan was standing by his locker with the Sherwood *Gazette* in his hand.

"Did you know there's half a page on you in this newspaper?!" Dylan waved the paper in the air. "And they put in a picture."

At practice on Tuesday, Peter hadn't said anything to any of the guys about the reporter talking to him. He had figured it all might go away if he didn't say anything. He glanced at the picture. It was a shot of him holding his MVP trophy.

The headline caption read *Northern Star Shines*.

The first line went on:

Peter Kuiksak from Tuktoyaktuk, Northwest

Territories, was instrumental in the Sherwood
Park Arrows gold-medal home-tournament victory on the weekend. The young lad, who is bil-
leting here so he can play hockey, not only won
MVP for every game the Arrows played, but
also captured the scoring title. According to
Peter, he's the best because, "I try hard."

Peter groaned. That opening quote sounded horrible.

"What's the matter?" said Dylan. "You're lucky. Your picture is in the newspaper. I've only been in a paper once."

"I didn't really say that." Peter pointed to the line with his
first quote.

"But you do try hard, it's true."

Suddenly the bell rang. Dylan handed Peter the paper. "You
can have this one. I've got two."

Peter shoved the paper between his binders and headed to
class.

The morning sped by and soon it was lunch. Peter hadn't had
a second to read the article. He couldn't just pull it out and read
it in front of everyone. On his way to the lunch room, he ducked
into the washroom. Closing the stall door, he sat on the toilet and
quietly pulled out the newspaper, hoping no one would hear him.
He was extremely careful not to rustle the pages.

Despite the first quote, the article was actually okay. When
he got to the part about Susie "being so supportive and his best
fan," Peter grinned. If he went to the library after lunch, he
might be able to scan the article and send it to Susie via e-mail.
And he definitely had to phone home again tonight.

When he finished reading, Peter flushed the toilet. With a
spring in his step, he made his way to the lunch room.

4

Dylan's Excitement

When Peter arrived at practice that night, Dylan was waiting for him at the front door of the arena. "Hey," Dylan said. "Sorry I missed you at lunch. I had a dentist appointment."

"That's okay." Peter had looked for Dylan only for a few seconds before he'd found other guys to sit with. Then he'd spent the rest of his lunch in the computer room.

"Did you read the article?" Dylan asked as he wheeled his bag down the hall, keeping stride with Peter.

"Yeah," replied Peter.

"I'd send it to my family if I were you."

"I already did. I scanned it at lunch."

"What did they say?"

"I haven't talked to them yet."

"My parents would be so proud. My mom would for sure send it to my grandma. She loves stuff like that."

Dylan trailed Peter into the dressing room. Peter saw an open seat and moved toward it, hoping Dylan would find somewhere else to sit. He didn't want to keep talking about the article, not in the dressing room. Dylan's attention over the article baffled Peter. Why did he care so much? Dylan followed Peter and plunked his bag down, forcing Matt to move down a little.

Peter hadn't even unzipped his bag when Dylan said, "Hey, did you guys see the Sherwood *Gazette* today?"

Peter kept his head down and pulled out his long underwear. His face felt hot in embarrassment.

"Nah," said Stu, stripping down to his boxers. "I don't read that paper."

"There's an article on how we won the tournament," said Dylan.

"Duh. They write about us every week," chirped Greg. "Anyway, it's not about us, it's about *him*." Greg jerked his head toward Peter. "And by the sounds of it, Mr. NWT is the only one who tries on this team. You're making us look bad," he said, turning to Peter.

"I didn't think the article was that bad," said Matt, shaking his head.

Peter remained silent as he strapped on his shin pads. He had no idea what to say.

"That reporter cut off one of my quotes too," Matt continued. "He was on a work term last year when it happened. Now they've hired him as a full-time sports writer. My dad says he'll get better, that he's fresh out of school and to give him a chance."

"My dad says if I worked as hard as NWT boy, they'd write about me too. I told him I don't want to be in that stupid paper. It's an embarrassment."

"None of this matters," said Stu, getting his goalie pads ready to put on. "I heard Coach is going to work us good tonight. We play against the St. Albert Flyers on Friday night, and if we beat them we move into first place."

"I'm ready to work," said Greg, "even though some people may not think so."

Peter didn't look up. He knew Greg was glaring at him.

* * *

Practice was really hard. Coach made them skate lines for twenty minutes before the practice and twenty minutes after. In between, they did two-on-one's and three-on-two's and lots of full-ice passing drills.

Peter's hair was soaked when he took off his helmet, but he felt good. There was nothing better than a good workout on the ice. At home, Peter always had the same feeling after a good hunt. On a hunt he lost track of time and became totally focused on the caribou. When he stepped on the ice to play hockey, he forgot about everything in his life and thought only about the puck. It was weird, because hockey was active and hunting was quiet, but they both gave him the same satisfied feeling. And he had to admit that scoring in hockey was by far the biggest thrill he had ever felt. Every time the puck went in the net, Peter's blood pumped in excitement. Sometimes on a hunt he got cold and wanted to go in, but he never tired of hockey.

"That was a good practice," said Coach in the dressing room. "I want everyone here an hour and a half before game time on Friday."

Totally exhausted, most of the guys leaned against the wall.

"Because you worked so hard tonight, tomorrow will be a light skate," said Coach.

Usually this news from Coach would have brought forth a cheer but everyone was so tired they could hardly speak. A few guys gave a pathetic "Yeah."

Coach smiled knowingly as he looked around the dressing room at the guys. "Eat well tonight, guys, to get some of your energy back. And," he paused and winked, "get that homework done."

All the guys groaned as Coach left the room. Peter was glad

Coach didn't mention anything about the article.

Finally, dressed and showered, Peter carried his bag toward the door. Dylan was right behind him.

"I'll meet you for lunch tomorrow," said Dylan as they walked down the hall.

"Sure." Peter was too tired to say anything else.

* * *

"Can I have your autograph?" asked Christine with a smirk when Peter entered the Patterson's kitchen.

"As if," replied Peter.

"Mom told me to tell you your dinner is in the oven."

"Thanks." Mrs. Patterson always left him generous portions. Peter opened the over door to see a plate heaped with chicken, mashed potatoes, and some sort of vegetable dish. Peter was so hungry he didn't care what was on the plate as long as it was food.

"Hey, all kidding aside," said Christine, "I thought it was a good picture of you."

"I thought I looked geeky." Peter got a knife and fork from the cutlery drawer. Did Christine really think he looked good in the picture?

"Well, you did a little, but I didn't want to say anything."

Peter glanced at her, shaking his head.

"What?" said Christine, laughing. "You have to admit the picture was kind of lame. The least they could have done was get you in action. What did the guys say?"

"Not much." Peter shovelled food in his mouth.

"What about that Dylan kid? He was telling everyone at school." She curved her mouth to make a funny face. Then she walked out of the room.

* * *

After he finished his homework, which took him two hours, Peter phoned home. Susie answered. "Hi, Susie," he said.

"How come you're calling so much?"

"Yesterday I forgot to ask how Baby Lisa is."

"She's good. She has two teeth now. She misses her Uncle Peter, though."

"I miss her too. She'll be so big when I see her next. Can she skate yet?"

Lisa laughed. "Peter, she's only five months old."

"Did you get my e-mail?"

"I didn't have to time to check today. I had to work a double shift because Karen had her baby."

"Boy or girl?" Peter doodled on a piece of paper.

"Boy. Maybe he'll be a hockey player."

"So you didn't see..." Peter paused for a beat. "The article was in the newspaper today."

"Are you kidding me? Already? Wait till I tell everyone. Edmonton is such a big city."

"You were mentioned," said Peter.

Susie giggled. "I thought you were lying to me yesterday. I can't believe my name is in a paper in Edmonton! Send it to me, okay? I'll show everyone."

"I did, in the e-mail."

"I'm gonna go check. You talk to Dad, okay?"

Peter heard the phone drop and bang on the floor, and he heard Susie yelling for his dad. Being in the newspaper was actually kind of cool if it made his sister happy.

5

Lots of Goals

A re you ready, Peter?" Mr. Patterson called up the stairs.

Even though Peter had been playing hockey for the Sherwood Park Arrows for three months, he still had a hard time tying a tie. In the city, Peter had found out, all the AAA teams had to dress up for games in good pants, shirts, and ties. He'd never owned a tie until he'd moved to Edmonton. Peter looked at his reflection in the mirror. The narrow end of his tie was way too long. He yanked it off and stuck it in his pocket. He'd have to redo it in the car. He slicked his hair with his hand one last time before he ran down the stairs.

After putting his equipment in the back of the van, Peter sat in the front passenger seat.

"This is a big game," said Mr. Patterson, backing out of the driveway.

"I can't wait to play," replied Peter. He pulled down the visor so he could check the mirror and fix his tie.

They drove the city streets in silence as Peter struggled with his tie. Finally, he snapped the visor back up and leaned back. His stomach lurched with its usual pre-game knots. By now Peter was used to the nerves and knew that once he was on the ice, they turned into adrenalin.

When they were five minutes from the arena, Mr. Patterson said, "You know, Peter, it was okay to talk to the reporter from the Sherwood Park paper. But if another reporter approaches you, it might be a good idea to have an adult with you when you answer questions."

"Why?" Peter didn't see what the big deal was.

"Sometimes it's just good to have someone with you. Every once in a while a reporter will twist your words. The pros have agents, you know, to help them."

"An agent?"

"An agent helps the player understand the signing of contracts, and guides a player when dealing with the media. Agents also work with players on their endorsement deals. Or they can sometimes help them get a scholarship at a college. Trevor has an agent now."

Peter glanced out the window. All of this talk was over his head. How much did it have to do with him? After all, he was only a Bantam hockey player. Trevor, the Patterson's oldest son, played Major Junior for the Red Deer Rebels.

Mr. Patterson patted Peter on the shoulder. "I think you might be creating a bit of a sensation."

"Sensation?" Peter frowned. "I don't want to do that. I just want to play good hockey."

Mr. Patterson steered the car into the arena parking lot as he said, "And that's exactly what you should do."

In the dressing room the Arrows talked about the hockey game — what they had to do to win, plays they'd practised, players they had to watch for, goalie weaknesses. Peter just listened. No one ever talked about plays up north in Tuk. Before the game, the guys threw tape and horsed around. All they talked about were girls and parties. Some guys even arrived just ten minutes before the puck dropped. When Peter came to Edmonton, he'd been surprised when Coach said they had to be so early for games. And he had no idea that he'd come to like the pre-game stuff so much. All the talk totally psyched him to play hockey.

For a good half hour before the game, Coach used his white board to go through the plays they had worked on in practice. Peter's heart beat like crazy as he listened intently to every word Coach had to say. He leaned forward and stared at the squiggly red lines on the board, not wanting to miss a thing. Coach reiterated the two-men-high, one-man-low play. And he harped on the defence to clear the puck. Stu needed the rest of team on top of their game to be successful in net. When Peter heard he was on the first line with Matt and Greg again, he felt his blood pumping through his veins.

Five minutes before game time, Peter rocked back and forth. He couldn't wait to get on the ice to get rid of the butterflies in his stomach. Finally, the door opened. The ice was ready.

Peter blasted onto the ice.

When the puck dropped, Peter slapped it back, but Dylan on defence missed it. The winger from the other team skated at full speed toward the puck. Peter whipped around and skated back. He would have to nail the guy.

The Flyers winger was heading wide. Peter pushed forward, trying to catch him. If he angled properly he could... Peter thrust his shoulder into the Flyers player and crushed him into the boards. Then he picked up the loose puck, saw Matt along the boards, and whacked it to him. Matt took off.

Peter trailed behind. He would be third man in, as Greg was just a step behind Matt on the other wing. Matt passed to Greg, who managed to slip around the Flyers defence. Peter sped over the blue line toward the net. He called to Greg.

But Greg decided he'd take a bad-angle shot. The goalie blocked it. Peter managed to get the end of his stick on the rebound and quickly passed to Matt. Matt fired off a shot, but the Flyers goalie made another brilliant save. This time Peter anticipated the rebound. When the puck landed on his tape, he one-timed it into the top corner. The goalie threw up his shoulder, but it was too late.

Peter threw his hands in the air in triumph.

"I can't believe he stopped my shot." Greg smacked his hands on the boards. "I should have scored."

"It doesn't matter," said Matt, swigging his water. "We're on the scoreboard."

"That's easy for you guys to say. You both picked up points," retorted Greg.

Matt eyed Greg, then shook his head. "Get over it."

By the end of the first period, Peter had two goals and one assist. Matt had scored the goal that Peter assisted on. The Arrows led 3–1.

As the Zamboni rolled in to clean the ice, the Arrows filed into the dressing room. Greg threw his helmet on the floor, angry that he hadn't picked up any points in the first period. Peter ignored him. Coach came in and talked to the team for a few minutes, then left. As team captain, Matt stood up and said, "We're winning this game. And we're doing it as a team. Every player in this room has done something to give us the lead. Now who's going to win this game?"

"Arrows. Arrows."

Peter made an effort to yell. Out of the corner of his eye he saw Greg snap his helmet on. His mouth wasn't moving in the chant.

On the bench, Peter heard Matt say to Greg, "Our line is on fire. You'll get points."

"If I'm with NWT boy I won't," hissed Greg. "My Dad is always comparing me to him. I wish he'd never come to play on our team."

Peter turned away. There was no way he would let Greg ruin his game. In fact, Greg's attitude made Peter more determined to play hard. After giving up so much to play hockey, Peter wasn't about to let anyone take away his dream.

* * *

When the buzzer announced the end of the game, the Arrows all jumped the bench and raced over to Stu, knocking him flat on the ice.

They had won 7–5.

In the dressing room, Dylan said to Peter, "You scored five goals! You're probably leading the league in scoring."

Peter untied his skate. "We work as a team. It doesn't matter who scores."

"I hate sitting on the bench," whispered Dylan.

Peter sat up and looked at Dylan. Coach had made Dylan sit the entire third period. "You can't let the scorers get by you. Talk to Coach about how you can cut them off better. You know, push them to the side so they can't get to the net."

Dylan nodded. "Hey, you want to do something this weekend? I might be able to get tickets for an Oilers game. They're playing Pittsburgh. I can't wait to see Sidney Crosby play."

"Awesome!" exclaimed Peter. He'd never been to a NHL hockey game.

As he left the dressing room, Dylan was right on his heels. Greg sat at the corner of the bench, scowling at Peter as he pushed open the door.

"I don't know why Greg's so mad," said Dylan when they

were walking down the hall. "I'd do anything to be on a line with you."

In the arena lobby, Mr. Patterson came up to Peter and said, "Great game, Peter. That's the way to put the puck in the net!"

"Thanks." He appreciated how Mr. Patterson was always so supportive, but was still uncomfortable being praised in front of a lot of people.

Peter looked around the lobby and saw Christine standing with a group of girls. When one of them saw Peter, she gave Christine's jacket a tug. Christine glanced in Peter's direction and gave her signature "I'm cool" Christine wave. The other girl put her hand to her mouth and giggled. Peter turned away, puzzled at what she was giggling about.

"I guess Christine's friends like to watch you play," said Mr. Patterson with a glint in his eyes.

"Not me," said Peter, shaking his head and turning. "They like Matt. Right, Dylan?"

But Dylan wasn't beside him anymore. "Where's Dylan?" he asked.

"At the canteen." Mr. Patterson gestured toward the lineup of people buying drinks and snacks. Then he patted Peter's shoulder. "I have to talk to your coach about something. I'll be right back."

Peter was left standing by himself. He had just started walking toward Dylan when he heard his name. It was Matt.

"What are you doing this weekend?" Matt asked.

"Not much."

"I might have an extra ticket to the Oilers game. I won't know until tomorrow, though. If I do, do you want to go?"

Matt had never asked Peter to go anywhere before. Matt was nice and said "hi" in the halls, but they didn't hang out after school or hockey. Matt was one of the most popular guys at school and had a big group of friends. Peter had yet to be included in that circle. "Uh, maybe," said Peter, thinking about how he missed his group of friends from home.

"I'll call you, okay? I gotta go. I have to see some of my friends who came to watch the game."

Peter watched Matt strut toward the door. Every one of Christine's friends also eyed him.

Suddenly, Dylan returned. "Here, I bought you a slurpie," he said.

* * *

Peter rode back home alone with Mr. Patterson. Christine had gone to a friend's house, and Andrew was with Mrs. Patterson.

"That was a big game for you, Peter."

Peter remained silent, not knowing how to answer the question. If he said, "Yeah," would that make him look like he thought he was good?

"When I left you in the lobby to talk to your coach, I was approached by another reporter." Mr. Patterson paused. "He heard about you and came to the game tonight. He was very impressed and wants to do a feature story on you. He asked if he could come to the house and take pictures. And he also wants to go to one of your practices. He said he got some good game shots tonight."

"A practice?" Peter squished his eyebrows together. "Does Coach know?"

"I made sure the reporter asked his permission."

"Will he come in the dressing room too?" How embarrassing.

"He might. I don't know all his ideas. I do know that he wants it to be a human-interest story."

"What does that mean?"

"He wants to write about you as a person, a boy coming from the North to play hockey. You have had a different minor hockey experience from that of most other kids."

"What paper is he from?" Peter undid his tie and shoved it in his coat pocket.

"The *Edmonton Sun*."

6

In Demand

A photographer is coming to our house!" Christine exclaimed at breakfast the next morning. She arched her eyebrows in surprise. "Wow, the *Edmonton Sun* never did a story like this when Trevor was the Bantam hot shot."

"Will he take pictures of us too?" Andrew poured way too much maple syrup on his French toast. "Peter and I could pretend we were playing mini-sticks or air hockey or—"

"You're dreaming, Andrew," interrupted Christine, taking the syrup from him. "Gross. Your French toast is floating. They don't want pictures of you."

"And they want them of you? Yeah, right. You'll probably take an hour to get ready and they won't even notice you." Andrew pretended to fling his hair over his shoulder.

"That's enough, you two," said Mr. Patterson, sipping coffee.

Peter lowered his head to eat the rest of his breakfast. What a commotion this reporter was causing! The guy had the okay to attend practice on Sunday, and he was coming to the house on Monday to take photos. Jeepers, he'd already phoned that morning to book the times.

"What are your plans for tonight, Christine?" Mrs. Patterson changed the topic.

"Bethany has an extra ticket for the Oilers game. Her brother can't go. I might go."

"I want to go to the game." Andrew pouted.

"You don't have a ticket." Christine stuck her tongue out at Andrew.

"What about you, Peter? Do you have plans?" Mrs. Patterson passed the last two pieces of French toast to Peter. "You can have the rest."

Peter plopped the toast on his plate. "I might be going to the Oilers game too," he mumbled.

"Peter, that's great! Your first NHL game," said Mr. Patterson. "I have tickets for January, so now you'll get to at least two games this year." He winked. "If the Oilers get in the playoffs, I'll get tickets for a game. That means you'll have to be here until the spring."

"Who are you going with?" Christine asked.

"I don't know. Maybe Dylan or Matt."

"Matt! Wow, you're hanging out with the popular guys now that you're in the newspaper, eh?"

If the whole Patterson family hadn't been at the table, Peter would have been tempted to tell Christine to mind her own business. Instead he quickly finished his breakfast, then excused himself and went to his room. Was that the reason why Matt had invited him to the game?

* * *

Dylan phoned first. "Still want to go to the game tonight? My dad says he'll pick you up at six, then we can watch the pregame skate."

"Sure." Peter told himself whoever called first would be the person he went to the game with. He kind of wished it had of been Matt, but an Oilers game was an Oilers game. Wait until he told the guys at home — and Susie, of course.

For the rest of the afternoon Peter did his homework. He hated school, but he had to at least pass to continue playing on the Arrows. Coach's wife helped him every Tuesday after school and it was making a huge difference, keeping him on track. In his bedroom, he kept looking at his clock radio, anxious for it to be time to leave. Time seemed to just crawl, and Peter wanted it to hurry up. Finally, he closed his books. He couldn't do any more homework. In the few minutes before Dylan arrived, Peter decided to phone home.

"Hey, Susie!" he said. "Guess what? I'm going to an Oilers game tonight."

"Are you serious?"

"One of the guys from my team has an extra ticket."

"You're so lucky, Peter."

"Maybe when you come to visit, I can get us tickets."

Susie didn't answer Peter.

"Susie, you still there?"

"Peter, I know you want me to come to Edmonton but... I've never been on a plane before." Her voice sounded small.

"Dad will be with you," said Peter quietly. He pictured Susie holding the phone in her hand, Baby Lisa at her feet. Susie had never even been to Yellowknife. The furthest she'd ever gone was Inuvik. She'd never travelled by anything but boat or car or snowmobile. "It's easier than going by boat," he said. "And faster."

"I'll think about it," she said. "Maybe I'll try." She paused then said, "Hey, have a good time tonight. Get me an autograph, okay?"

"Who do you want? They're playing Pittsburgh."

"Really? Get Sidney Crosby for me if you can."

When Peter hung up the phone, he realized he'd forgotten to tell Susie about the reporter from the *Edmonton Sun*. She had been so excited with the last article he'd sent her, he was sure she'd be thrilled to see something in a big newspaper. When it was printed, he'd surprise her and send it.

Peter had just hung up the phone when it rang. With all the calls coming into the Patterson household, it was rarely for Peter, so he didn't answer it.

"Peter," Mrs. Patterson called up the stairs. "The phone is for you."

Peter lifted the receiver. He still couldn't believe that he had a phone in his room. At home in Tuk, they had just one phone for everyone.

"Hey, Peter." It was Matt.

"Hey."

"You still want to go to the game?"

"I told Dylan I'd go with him."

Matt paused before he said, "Cool. I can ask someone else. Let's meet between periods."

7

Oilers Game

The front of the arena was packed with people. Scalpers walked around outside, hawking tickets. "Tickets, tickets, who needs a ticket?"

Peter stared in amazement at the entire scene as he followed Dylan and his dad.

Lots of fans were dressed up in Oilers jerseys, Oilers hoodies, and Oilers ball caps. A few fans wore the black and yellow Pittsburgh jerseys, but they were definitely outnumbered, and were loudly heckled by the Oilers fans. Some fans had brought long blue horns. Peter couldn't believe the noise they made. And there were fans that had painted their entire faces with the blue, white, and orange Oilers colours.

How did they do that? Peter figured it would have taken them hours to paint their faces. He was so in awe and so intent on gawking at all the commotion that he stepped on Dylan's heels a few times.

Dylan laughed. "Stop stepping on my shoes."

"Sorry," said Peter. He widened his smile. "This is amazing."

"I know, isn't it awesome?" said Dylan. "Can you imagine having all these fans come to watch you play? That would be the coolest thing ever."

A tingle ran up and down Peter's spine. *That would be the coolest thing ever.* The noise around him had his heart beating faster. Peter tried to absorb everything.

Inside the arena Dylan and Peter dodged the crowd to find their seats. When Peter walked into the arena, he stopped and held his breath. The ice surface looked so big!

An usher wearing a green uniform took their tickets. Then he pointed to their seats. They walked down the stairs.

"I can't wait to watch the warm-up," said Dylan.

Peter didn't reply as his head swivelled around. But when the players came on the ice, Peter immediately leaned forward, intent on watching the warm-up. He wanted to pinch himself. Was he really at an NHL game? This was too good to be true.

He watched them skate and shoot on the goalie. "They're so good," said Peter. "Their shots are so hard."

"You'll be that good one day," said Dylan. "Even my dad said so, in the car the other day."

Peter shivered. Was it really possible for him to think that he might play in the NHL?

As the practice wound down, the players started heading for their dressing rooms. Mesmerized, Peter sat in his seat until the last player had left the ice. Then he looked around the rink at all the seats. They went up and up and up. He craned his neck to look up at the top row. People paid money to watch from there? How could they see the game? Peter shook his head. He knew the game tonight was sold out.

"Every seat in this arena will be filled," he said to Dylan, still looking at all the seats. "I wonder what it would be like to play in front of so many people."

"It would be so cool." Dylan also looked longingly around the arena. "Ever since I was little, my dream has been to play in the NHL." Dylan sighed.

Peter glanced at Dylan, knowing this year had been tough for him. Was he struggling with his dream now? When Peter was little, living in Tuk, he'd never had the dream of playing in the NHL. Now, seeing this huge rink, he couldn't think of anything he wanted to do more.

"You'll make it," he said to Dylan.

"I hope so," replied Dylan. "My dad says I have to keep trying." Dylan stood. "Hey, let's go look at the T-shirts and stuff. And get some food."

"We're supposed to meet Matt in between periods." Peter and Dylan ran up the arena stairs.

"Really?" Dylan's eyes lit up. "Did he call you?"

"He asked if I wanted to go to the game with him, but I said I was going with you."

"Wow," said Dylan quietly. "Thanks."

Peter smiled at Dylan, but was puzzled by his reaction. After looking at all the Oilers paraphernalia — Peter really wished he had the money to buy everyone in his family a jersey — he bought an action picture of Sydney Crosby for Susie and a little Oilers T-shirt for baby Lisa. He also picked up some Oilers decals for his brothers and a key chain for his dad. He sure hoped he could get an autograph at the end of the game. Dylan's father had agreed to let them stay late, to wait as the players came out.

After looking at everything in the store, they got in line for food. Peter bought nachos and cheese and Dylan got a hot dog.

Finally, back in their seats, it was game time.

The arena went black. The crowd started to cheer. Then the strobe lights and the loud music started up.

The lyrics to the song were, "We will! We will! Rock You!" Peter had heard it a hundred times — they even played it when the Arrows played — but tonight, for some reason, the music gave him goose bumps. He sucked in a deep breath and sat forward.

The referees and linemen skated onto the ice. The strobe lights followed them.

Then, in a super-loud voice, the announcer called out, "Are you ready to rumble?"

The song changed and the music suddenly got louder. Peter couldn't sit another minute. As he stood, he watched the Oilers blast onto the dark ice, a light following each of them.

"Here's our starting lineup for tonight's game!" By now the announcer's voice was at a fevered pitch. The fans burst into applause. There were so many people in the arena, the noise was unbelievable. Wide-eyed, Peter stared at the players.

After each player in the starting lineup for the Oilers was named to huge cheers, the lights came on. Then the crowd went wild with cheers and boos because the young star of the Pittsburgh Penguins was on the ice — Sidney Crosby.

The arena hushed when a man stepped onto the ice with a microphone. He sang both the American and Canadian national anthems. Near the end of the Canadian anthem, the crowd started to yell again. Peter's body tingled in excitement.

When the puck finally dropped to start the game, both teams moved at full throttle.

"They're playing third-man back too," Peter said to Dylan.

"I saw that. Their defence really pinch, don't they?"

"Yeah," Peter replied without taking his eyes off the ice. "Pronger is fast, so he can pinch. Check the size of him."

"St. Louis isn't big though. He's smaller than you. But tough."

By the end of the first period, the Oilers were leading 2–1. "Come on," said Dylan. "Let's go find Matt."

Peter trailed Dylan up the stairs. They had to swerve through the crowd to get to the pizza place where Matt told Peter to meet him. When Matt saw them, he waved. He was standing with Greg and a guy Peter recognized from school as a player on the basketball team.

"What a great game!" Matt exclaimed.

"Did you see Smyth do that wrap-around?" Peter pretended he was stick-handling. "That was so sweet. He ducked the puck underneath."

"He's amazing," said Greg. He pretended to do a wrist shot. "He's so fast at one-timers. And every time he does the wrap-around, it works."

Peter glanced at Greg. Off the ice and out of the dressing room, he was actually kind of friendly.

"How about Pronger?" Matt's eyes were wide with admiration. "That guy's slapshot from the point is like a bullet."

"And Crosby," exclaimed Peter.

"Yeah, Crosby." Matt responded to Peter. "Man, can you imagine being as good as him?"

"I read he was on the youngest player ever to be picked for the Canadian World Junior team," said Greg. "My dad went to a fundraising dinner where they were auctioning a Crosby jersey from when he played for Quebec. He paid like a thousand dollars for it. My mom was really mad at him."

"Your house is like a museum with hockey stuff," said Matt. "Don't you have a pair of Mario Lemieux's skates?"

"Yeah. My dad loves anything NHL."

"I'd do anything to make the NHL," said Matt, "and have someone pay big bucks for my jersey. Can you imagine playing in front of so many people and being so good? And signing autographs for everyone. Have you ever seen the people that wait by the door at the end of a game? It would be cool to be so famous."

What it would be like to have people wait for me after I finished playing a game? Peter thought to himself.

8

Cheap Shot

At breakfast the next morning, all Peter could think about was the reporter coming to practice later. His stomach was so upset, he could only pick at his food. He tried to remember how the NHL players had handled everyone shoving papers to get autographs last night after the game. None of them would be worried about a newspaper reporter. Peter decided he had to rise to the occasion. Coach always used that statement before a big game. Peter finished his breakfast and got ready for practice.

Squaring his shoulders in anticipation, Peter stood outside the dressing room. He tapped his foot and took a deep ragged breath before pushing open the door. The reporter had wanted a shot of him carrying his bag into the dressing room. As soon as he entered, he heard the camera click. Then he heard another click, and another. The guy kept taking shots. Peter stared straight ahead. When an open spot on the bench entered his field of vision, he wheeled his bag over.

The dressing room was unusually quiet. No one threw tape or horsed around.

Peter unzipped his bag. The reporter knelt in front of him

and took a close-up of his face. Peter froze.

"Just go through you normal routine," said the reporter, looking through the lens of his camera. "I just need another couple of shots in here."

Peter pulled out his equipment. How was he supposed to get dressed? He couldn't strip down in front of a camera. Fortunately, before Peter could panic, the reporter stood and brushed off his knees.

"Thanks," he said. "That's all I need in here." Then he left. In record time, Peter undressed and slipped on his under clothing.

Suddenly the quiet dressing room was buzzing with noise.

"Where's he from?" Dylan asked.

"The *Sun*," mumbled Peter. He kept his head down and strapped on his shin pads. Everyone was staring at him.

"The *Sun*," said Stu. "Wow. You're in the big time."

Matt stood up. "Hey, guys," he said. "This is great for our team. And Peter deserves some recognition. He scored five goals the other night."

"Why didn't you say anything about this last night?" mumbled Greg. "A little advanced warning would have been nice."

* * *

The reporter set up in the stands and took shots for the first fifteen minutes of the practice. Then he packed up and left. Instantly, a wash of relief flowed over Peter. Now he could give his full attention to the drills.

During the rest of practice, Peter had this funny feeling that Greg was out to get him. He kept hitting Peter after the play — even after the whistle. But he was sneaky and did it when Coach wasn't looking. Once Peter saw Greg glance at his father in the stands. His father gave him the thumbs-up.

Although Peter tried to ignore the cheap shots, they were starting to bug him. Finally, he found an opportunity to check Greg. He lined Greg up and gave him a good solid hit, thrusting his body, sending him flying into the boards and to the ice. When Greg was down, he stuck out his stick and tried to trip Peter. Peter nimbly jumped over the stick.

Greg stood up, adjusted his helmet, and glared at Peter. "You just wait," he said.

With just five minutes left in the practice, Coach announced that they could scrimmage. Everyone cheered. They threw sticks in the middle of the ice to make the teams. Peter didn't care who was on his team, he just wanted to scrimmage.

Whenever the Arrows scrimmaged the play was super intense, and there were no whistles. Coach told them to keep the play moving, as creative play was necessary to become a good hockey player. That's what the scrimmages were for, to try new things.

Coach dropped the puck and Peter smacked it over to Matt. Matt took off up the boards. Peter hustled forward. He wanted to try the move he had seen Ryan Smyth do the night before. At the back of the net, he tapped his stick on the ice. Matt saw him and fired the puck to him. Peter was about to swing around when he felt a stick hit him hard across the back. Peter went flying forward, falling face-first on the ice.

His head snapped back. He gasped for breath. Stars swirled in front of his face. He lay still for a moment, unable to get up. He heard the whistle, but it seemed to be far away.

"Peter, can you hear me?"

Peter slowly opened his eyes. His vision was blurred. Coach leaned over him.

"I don't want to roll you over, Peter. Can you wiggle your toes and fingers?"

Peter did, and he could feel them. He nodded. Then he

slowly tried to get up on all fours. He stayed there for a few seconds, knowing he was wobbly. Finally, he tried to stand.

Coach held his arm. "Let me help you."

Usually Peter would shrug off assistance, but today he instinctively knew he needed help to keep from collapsing on the ice.

Coach helped him to his feet. All the guys tapped their sticks on the ice.

Disorientated and dizzy, Peter let Coach help him to the bench. Immediately, Peter sat down. Coach handed him his water bottle. "Take a sip," he said.

Peter swigged some water. Then he put his head between his legs to thwart the nauseous feelings. All the guys had skated in to surround him.

"Hit the showers," said Coach to the rest of the guys. "And no one leave."

Peter sat on the bench for a few more minutes, his legs shaking. He watched the Zamboni go around the rink a few times. Finally, he stood up. "I'm okay," he said.

"You sure?" asked Coach.

"Yeah, I'm fine."

Coach patted him on the back. "You may want to take it easy for the rest of the day. You took a pretty hard knock."

The talk all hushed when Peter entered. He could feel the tension fill the dressing room. He showered and dressed without saying a word to anyone. All the guys were in street clothes when Coach entered.

"Okay, guys. Listen up." He paused. "Rough-housing is okay. Cheap shots are not. I don't want to see that kind of hit ever again. You cheap shot one of your own players in practice and you will be suspended, just like in a real game. Got that straight?"

As soon as Coach left, Peter headed for the door, wanting to exit as quickly as possible. He lugged his bag down the hallway. Mr. Patterson was deep in conversation with Coach John when Peter entered the arena lobby. By the way they glanced his way, he knew they were talking about him.

Peter went right to the front doors to wait for Mr. Patterson. Someone approached him and Peter turned, hoping to see Dylan or Matt. Instead, it was Greg.

"That will teach you to mess with me, NWT boy," hissed Greg.

Peter heard a voice from the distance. "Come on, Greg. Let's go home."

When Peter glanced toward the voice, he saw Greg's dad with a grin plastered across his face.

9

Peter in *The Sun*

Mrs. Patterson cleaned the house for two hours the next day. She vacuumed and dusted and swished out the toilets. Christine spent an hour straightening her hair and doing her makeup. Andrew ran around, excited. Peter couldn't believe all the fuss. After yesterday's incident, Matt had called to ask if Peter was okay. He wanted Peter to know that the rest of the guys were okay with the newspaper article, no matter how Greg was acting.

The reporter stayed in the Patterson's home for more than two hours. He asked questions of everyone and talked to Peter for a good half hour. Then he took photos of Peter with the family, of Peter with his Inuit drum, of Peter doing his homework. Peter couldn't figure out why. *Why did the guy want so many pictures? This was supposed to be a hockey story.*

When the reporter finally left, Peter felt exhausted and cranky. It had been harder than playing hockey, or even doing school work. But it wasn't as if he'd exerted any energy, like he would at a hard practice.

Mr. Patterson put his arm on Peter's shoulder. "You did great, Peter. You must be glad it's over."

"I like the hockey part way better."

Mr. Patterson laughed. "That's my boy." He tousled Peter's hair.

Peter couldn't help but smile.

"You have another big game coming up," said Mr. Patterson.

"Coach says Olds is the team to beat," replied Peter, feeling some of the tension leave his shoulders. "I've heard from some of the guys that they have one player who is really good. He's even better than that Kevin Jennings I went to camp with in the summer."

"I have a feeling there may be some scouts and agents at this game," said Mr. Patterson with a glint in his eye. "Trevor wants us to pick him up in Red Deer so he can come and watch too." He patted Peter on the back. "On Sunday afternoon Trevor has a home game, so we're going to book a hotel room for Saturday night. Instead of driving back, we can all stay and go to the game."

"Cool," said Peter. After his experience at the NHL game, Peter was excited to see any big game.

Mr. Patterson winked. "And I'll get Trevor to take you down to the dressing room too."

"Really?" Peter said in excitement.

"You know, Peter," Mr. Patterson suddenly looked rather serious. "I'm sure the scouts will be looking at some other players too. Maybe a couple of you guys from the Arrows."

* * *

The week flew by. Everyday Peter checked the *Edmonton Sun* for the article, but it wasn't there. At practice, Peter made a point of avoiding Greg. Greg seemed to avoid Peter too. He didn't go out of his way to make nasty comments or take cheap shots. Maybe what Coach said got through to him. But Peter also noticed that Greg's dad wasn't at the arena. Matt told Peter that Greg's father was out of town on business.

On Thursday, when Peter showed up at school, his teacher met him in the hall. "Peter, that was some article on you," she said.

"What do you mean?" He furrowed his eyebrows.

"In the *Edmonton Sun* this morning there's a full-page article on you." She paused. "There's a copy of the paper in the office if you want to take a look."

Peter rushed into the office. When he saw his face in the top corner of the front page he was shocked.

He was the highlight for the sports section.

Immediately, he opened up the paper. His eyes grew wide when he saw all the pictures. There was an action shot of him, one of him entering the dressing room, one with all the Pattersons, and one with him playing his Inuit drum for Christine and Andrew.

The story focused on his life at the Pattersons', and most of the quotes were from the questions the reporter had asked about his life in Edmonton. They mentioned a little about his home in Tuktoyaktuk and about his family. But, unlike the article in the Sherwood *Gazette*, that certainly was not the focus. The reporter quoted Christine and Andrew about what it was like to have a billet from the Northwest Territories and what they were learning about Northern culture. Peter had to admit that Christine looked good in the photos.

When he felt a hand on his shoulder, he jumped. "That's quite a spread." It was the principal of the school, Mr. Howe.

"I, uh, guess so," said Peter, not sure how to answer. The principal had never talked to him before. Peter knew Mr. Howe was a big hockey fan, but had never had the opportunity to actually talk to him.

"You should be proud of yourself," said Mr. Howe. "We're certainly proud to have you at our school. And from what I understand, you're working hard on your studies. That's to be commended, Peter."

Peter smiled shyly. A part of him felt slightly embarrassed and totally bewildered to be the center of such attention, but... a part of him really liked it too. It was a kick to see his picture in the paper.

Mr. Howe patted him on the back just as the bell rang. "Time for class."

The other students were nattering as usual when Peter entered his classroom. But suddenly, everyone stopped talking and turned to stare at him. Then, to Peter's surprise, Tessa, the most popular girl in the grade said, "You looked good in the newspaper, Peter."

The heat rushed to Peter's cheeks and he hurried to his seat. Once he was sitting, he opened his books, lowered his head, and pretended to read. He felt a tap on his shoulder. At first he ignored it, knowing it was Erin, the girl who sat behind him. But she tapped again and whispered, "Hey, Peter."

He turned just slightly, so he could answer but not have to actually look at the girl. "What?" he whispered.

"I agree with Tessa. They put in some good pictures of you."

Peter buried his nose back in his books. *Girls never talk to me, not at this school.* He pulled out his pen and began writing to make it look as if he was busy. *She is a hottie too.* The teacher started talking and Peter breathed a sigh of relief.

Near the end of English period, the teacher announced that they were going to be doing group projects to study the novel *Holes* by Louis Sacher.

Peter hated this part of school. A month back, they'd had to do a group project in Social Studies and he'd ended up working with the kids no one wanted to work with. It had turned out okay, as one kid was a fabulous artist and did all the drawings. They'd received a good mark, and Peter told himself he didn't really care who he worked with, as long as he got a good mark so he could continue playing hockey.

"I want you in groups by next class," said the teacher just as the bell rang to signify locker break. "Two is enough, but if you want to work with three, that's fine. I'll give out the topics next class, so you need to read at least the first three chapters."

Peter slowly put his novel into his binder and packed up his books, hoping to give all the other kids time to get out of the classroom. If he was the last one out, he wouldn't have to talk to anyone.

At his locker, he clicked open the lock and piled his books on the top shelf, pulling out his gym shorts, T-shirt, and running shoes. Gym was definitely his favourite class.

"Hey, Peter," said Tessa. He turned to find her standing behind him. Beside her was Erin.

Tessa had long red hair and was the captain of the volley-ball team. She was almost as tall as Peter. Everyone liked Tessa, or at least that's how it seemed to Peter. She wasn't snotty, like the girls who walked down the hall flinging their hair over their shoulders all the time. Peter knew Matt liked Tessa because he talked about her in the dressing room, saying she was the hottest girl in the school. Erin, in contrast, was tiny and blond and laughed all the time. Peter found himself with the two most popular girls in his grade.

"Um, what?" He had no idea what to say. These girls had never spoken to him before.

"Do you want to be our partner for the English project?"

Peter shrugged because he was tongue-tied. Since he'd been in Edmonton he'd hardly talked to girls … except Christine. "I'm not… that good at English." *What a lame thing to say,* he thought. Why couldn't he have come up with something witty and funny, like Matt would have?

Tessa smiled at him anyway and Erin giggled. "Peter, we wouldn't ask you if we didn't want to work with you."

Peter knew both girls managed to get great grades and were honour students. He'd be crazy not to partner with them on this project; he needed all the marks he could get.

"Okay, sure," he said.

"We should meet tomorrow, in the library at lunch," said Tessa. "I can't today, because I have a volleyball meeting." Tessa turned to Erin. "Can you make it tomorrow?"

"Yup." She smiled her perfect smile. Peter looked away so he wouldn't get caught staring.

"I'll meet you just after I eat," Peter mumbled. He rummaged for something — anything — in his locker. He pulled out a pencil.

"Sounds good. I'll do some prep work tonight," said Tessa.

"Yeah, me too," said Erin bobbing her head. Her long blond hair fell halfway down her back. "When's your next game, Peter?" she asked.

"We play in Olds on the weekend." Peter stared at the pencil in his hand.

"Hey, maybe I'll come to your next home game." Erin turned to Tessa. "We better get going or we're going to be late for math." She turned again to face Peter. "See ya."

The girls took off down the hall at a fast clip, leaving Peter alone at his locker. He watched them walk away, unable to take his eyes off them. *Am I really going to work on a project with two popular girls?* He wondered. Was it because he was in the newspaper? If it was, then he hoped to get in the paper some more. Wait until he told the guys at home.

In Peter's gym class, a few kids he didn't know made comments about the article, as did the gym teacher. Dylan stuck by his side for the entire class and begged Peter to be his badminton partner. When gym class was over, Dylan ran to catch up with Peter in the hall. "Wait at your locker for me, okay?" he said.

"I'll just meet you in the lunch room," replied Peter.

"I'll be quick," said Dylan. "Wait for me."

Standing by his locker, Peter couldn't figure out why Dylan wanted him to wait. They always met in the lunch room. He tapped his foot, agitated. Peter was starving and wanted to eat. By now the cafeteria line for drinks would be really long. Finally, Peter saw Dylan running down the hall, almost out of breath.

"Sorry," he said.

"Whatever."

"I can't believe they did such a big article on you in the *Edmonton Sun*. So many people are talking about it."

"Like who?" asked Peter. Maybe more girls!

"I dunno," said Dylan. "Just, like, lots of people. I had a few guys ask me if you were as good as the article said."

Peter glanced at Dylan. "There are lots of good guys on our team."

"Yeah. But, come on, you're the best. You're leading the league in scoring."

As soon as Peter and Dylan walked into the lunch room, Peter heard his name. He stopped, surprised. No one ever called Peter's name in the lunch room.

"Peter!" Matt stood on the bench, even though it was against cafeteria rules. He waved. "Over here. Come sit with us."

Dylan pushed Peter forward. "Come on," he said. "Let's join them."

When Peter turned to look at Dylan, he noticed that his eyes were wide with excitement. For some reason, it made Peter feel funny.

10

Signing Autographs

Practice was scheduled for after school. Peter rushed off the bus and ran to the Pattersons'. Christine was staying late at school for volleyball practice.

In the kitchen, Peter snatched at apple from the fruit bowl and sliced a big hunk of cheese to eat. He was always starving after school.

"How was school?" Mrs. Patterson pointed to a pot on the stove when she walked into the kitchen. "I've made hamburger soup. Do you want a quick bowl?" She glanced up at the kitchen clock hanging above the sink. "You have a few minutes before we have to leave."

"Sure," said Peter.

As she ladled him a bowl of soup, she said, "Did you see the paper today?"

"Yeah." He took the soup and sat down at the kitchen table.

"I've phoned some friends and asked them to save me copies. You'll have to send one home." She handed him a sleeve of crackers. Peter crunched the crackers and dropped them in his bowl of soup.

The back door flew open and Andrew, totally out of breath, ran into the kitchen. "Did you see the paper?" His eyes gleamed.

Mrs. Patterson laughed.

"I've never been in the paper before. My teacher showed it to my class." He turned to look at Peter. "All my friends want your autograph. They say if they get it now, when you're big star it will be worth a lot of money!"

* * *

"Peter, can I talk to you?" said Coach when Peter arrived at the arena.

Peter moved to one side of the hallway.

Coach placed a hand on Peter's shoulder and looked him in the eyes. "How are you doing?"

"O-kay." Peter looked around, shifty-eyed. Why was Coach asking him that? He had phoned after Greg's hit and Peter told him he was fine. Maybe it wasn't about his physical condition?

"You've had a lot of adjustments in the last few months. Now you're starting to get recognized for how well you're playing," Coach continued. He paused. "It's not always easy to be the centre of attention."

"So far it's okay."

So, this was about the newspaper article. Everyone was making such a big deal out of it and Peter couldn't figure out why. Most of the attention so far had been kind of neat — two popular girls asked him to work on a project with them, and he'd had lots of guys to sit with at lunch.

"People will react to your success in different ways." Coach paused before he said, "I'm here if you ever want to talk."

Peter nodded, then headed to the dressing room. He doubted

he would ever have to talk to the Coach or anyone about this.

The music blared when Peter entered the dressing room. He saw Greg and purposely sat on the bench on the other side of the room. No one said anything about the article. Peter, for some weird reason, felt a stab of disappointment. He thought for sure Matt would have made an announcement. After all, it was the *Edmonton Sun*.

Coach started the practice with skating, telling the team he was going to work them hard to get ready for the next few games and the big tournament at Christmas. They skated circles without pucks, then they skated with pucks. Next, they did tight turns around the cones, and after that they did zigzags from line to line. Once the warm-up was over, he called them in to the white board.

"Okay, listen up," he said. "We've got a big game this weekend. We're playing the Olds Lions. They are undefeated." He looked around at the team. "Guys, you can beat them if you play your game. Defence, today we're going to work on pinching. I want you to be aggressive. Forwards, if your defence pinch, you have to be prepared to back-check. Thus, all the skating." He paused and the silence was such that Peter could hear everyone breathing.

Coach continued, "I can honestly say, this is the first time I've had total confidence in a team that I want to teach the pinch. You're the fastest team I've ever coached." He picked up his marker and started drawing on the white board. "We're going to do a two-on-two back-check drill to start off. I want you to read the rush, and I want the defensive forward to track back." He drew squiggly lines on the board. "That forward has to gain a defensive position on the back check. If our forwards become lazy on this kind of play, we will give our opposition breakaways. Mark my words, they'll send a guy to the middle.

And we don't want that."

Matt held up his hand.

"Go ahead, Matt," said Coach.

"Coach is right, we do have a fast team," he said with assurance. "But we have to work together. If we don't work as a team, we won't win. Every guy is a part of this team."

Coach nodded. "Thanks, Matt." Then he said, "Remember defence-zone coverage and positioning — and most of all your DZone responsibilities and defensive support. Okay, let's go!"

Everyone hustled to get into position. Peter could feel his adrenalin pumping. He could tell, from the way every player rushed to position, that he wasn't the only one inspired by Coach John's and Matt's speech.

The fast pace of the practice left Peter breathless. For the full hour everyone played at a fevered pitch, giving 100 percent. By the time it was over, Peter was soaked in sweat.

In the dressing room, every guy was raring to play on the weekend. No one said a word about the newspaper article, which was fine by Peter. They had only one more practice, and Coach said it would be a light skate with an emphasis on shooting, to prepare the goalies for the big game. He also wanted to work on the neutral-zone chip pass to push the puck forward for good offence. At first, when Coach used hockey lingo like "DZone" and "NZone," Peter hadn't had a clue what he was talking about. Matt had sensed his confusion and took the time to explain. Now Peter used the words in regular sentences.

By seven o'clock, Peter was back at the Pattersons'. As soon as he walked in the door, Andrew ran over to him. "My friends are here. They're all downstairs waiting for you."

"You were serious?" Peter squinted in shock.

"Yeah, come on."

Peter really felt silly. Signing autographs was for the pro

players. But Andrew tugged on his shirt. "You have to come downstairs."

"Well, okay."

"What are you okaying now?" Christine stood in the doorway. Peter hadn't heard her approach from the hall.

"Nothing," he said.

"My friends are here and they want Peter's autograph," piped up Andrew. "They all say that when he's really, really rich and, like, wins the NHL Rookie of the Year award, this autograph will be worth tons of money."

Christine doubled over in laughter. She was almost choking when she said, "You've got to be kidding. You really invited your friends over for his autograph? How much are you charging them?"

Andrew scrunched up his face in a huge pout.

"You're charging your friends?" Peter stared at Andrew in astonishment.

Andrew puckered his lips and looked away. "Just a dollar," he squeaked out. He paused, then looked back at Peter and said in his best little-kid pleading voice, "Please, Peter. Please."

"If there's a way to make money without doing work, Andrew smells it out," said Christine, shaking her head. "He did this with Trevor too."

"Did Trevor, uh, do the autographs?" Peter needed to find out what to do.

"Of course," said Christine. "He thought it was cool." She smiled. "Go ahead. Make those little twerps happy. I hope you invited over different kids this time, Andrew, or else they're going to see through your stupid little money-making venture." With that she left the room.

"Do your friends have pens?" Peter asked Andrew.

"Yup," said Andrew. "And they each have the article from

the newspaper. Each one will tell you where you should sign."

"I'll be down in a minute." Peter gave Andrew a half-smile as he shook his head.

Andrew punched the air with his fist. "Yes," he said. Then he ran from the room.

Peter took the stairs two at a time to get to his bedroom. He rifled in his desk to find a pen and a piece of paper. At first he wrote his name slowly. Then he stopped to see what it looked like. How was he supposed to make it look good? He tried a few more times until he was sort of satisfied. Still embarrassed, he went downstairs.

The five boys cheered when he hit the bottom stair. Christine was at the computer, and she turned to look at Peter with a big smirk on her face. "Should I bow now or later?"

"I'm first," said one of the boys.

"I'm next." Another boy pushed to the front.

The boys lined up and Peter wrote his name for them. When he was finished, Andrew was beaming. "Thanks, Peter. You're the greatest."

11

City Girls

Peter was finishing off his homework when a knock sounded on his door. "Come in," he said.

Christine pushed open his door. "How's your arm?"

Peter frowned. "My arm? What are you talking about?"

"I thought it might be sore from signing all those autographs."

Peter glared at her. "Whatever."

"Hey, listen," she said. "I heard a rumour that Tessa asked you to be her partner for a project."

"So?"

"I think she likes you."

"She likes Matt. And anyway, it wasn't just Tessa. We have three in the group." Peter picked up his pen and returned to his work. Was Christine right? Did Tessa like him? Peter shook his head. It couldn't be true. Butterflies flew in Peter's stomach.

"I don't know about that." Christine stepped toward Peter's desk. "Tessa always likes the guy she thinks is the best athlete. Be careful."

Peter glanced at Christine. Why was she telling him this?

What difference did it make to her? Peter's face flushed. City girls were so different from his girl friends in Tuk. "I've only ever said two words to her," he replied. "I don't get why I should be careful."

"Because I know her. I've played on teams with her." She paused before she asked, "Did you like the article in the *Sun*?"

"It was okay," Peter nodded.

"I got asked to go to a movie on Friday because of it." Christine didn't look too happy.

"Isn't that good?"

"Not really. I like guys to like me for who I am, not who billets at my house."

"Sorry."

"It's not your fault. It's just so annoying."

* * *

By the end of the next day, Christine was steaming mad with all the people who were asking her what she was doing on the weekend. She stormed onto the bus and plunked down on the seat beside Peter.

"I can't believe it. At lunchtime volleyball practice, Tessa asked me point blank if she could come to Olds with us on the weekend." She scowled when she turned to look at Peter. "I hardly know her! I play volleyball with her but that's about it. *She's in grade eight!*"

Peter remained silent. He'd met Tessa and Erin at break to work on the project, and they'd had a fun time.

"Did she say anything to you about this?" Christine persisted.

"We talked about our project but, that's all."

"Are you sure?"

Peter glanced out the window before he answered. "I think I'm sure."

"So she did say something to you." Christine's eyes smoldered with anger. "Tell me. What did she say?" Her voice was demanding.

Peter traced his finger along his jeans. "Nothing really. She just asked where I was playing and if you were going. I said I thought so."

Christine groaned. "Peter, you are so thick sometimes. She asked you those questions to get you to ask her to come along with us. She has such nerve. I told her she couldn't come because I've already asked Jemma."

Peter leaned his head against the bus window. He obviously had no idea how girls operated. Tessa seemed so fun and nice. Erin did too. He liked them both.

Peter and Christine didn't talk the rest of way home. He let her fume in silence. They were greeted by Andrew when they walked in the back door.

"Man, oh, man, did I have to take a lot of messages for you guys." He waved a piece of paper in front of their faces, jerking it back when Christine reached for it. "It might cost you," said Andrew.

Christine snatched the paper out of his hand. "I'm not in the mood for your games, Andrew."

"Whoa. Crab-by."

Christine scanned the names, then shook her head. "I am not friends with any of these people." She furiously shook her head. "They think they can get to Peter through me."

She thrust the paper at Peter. He had no idea what to do with it. In fact, he wasn't sure he even wanted to see the list. None of this made any sense to him. Why would anyone who didn't know him want to get to him through Christine?

"There are only three names here," he said. "It's not that big a deal."

"To me, it is," said Christine. "I can't stand people who are hockey wanna-be fans. You either like hockey or you don't. And you either like someone or you don't. You don't decide to be friends with people just because they're in the newspaper and famous."

"I'm hardly famous," said Peter. "Only two articles have been written on me."

"Right now, everyone at school is talking about you." She grabbed the paper from Peter's hands, ripped it up, and threw it in the garbage. "This kind of people infuriate me." Then she stalked out of the room, her footsteps hard on the floor.

Peter stood still, staring after Christine, wondering if what she said was true. Was everyone talking about him? He shoved his hands in his pockets. Having the other students talk about him was far better than being teased, that was for sure.

Andrew patted Peter on the shoulder and said, "Don't worry. She'll get over it." Then he smiled impishly. "You wanna game of mini-sticks?"

* * *

That night, Dylan phoned to talk. Peter didn't really like talking on the phone, and he didn't have much to say. Although Peter liked Dylan, he hoped he wouldn't start phoning him every night.

Peter had just hung up the phone when it rang again. He picked up the receiver. Maybe it was his dad. "Hello."

"Peter, hi. It's Tessa."

"Hey," he said to Tessa. No girl had ever called him at the Pattersons' house. He wound the phone cord around his finger.

"I just wanted to tell you I was online doing some research for our project," she said. "I found the author's website. And it explained how the movie *Holes* was made into a movie, what the author had to go through. That's exactly our topic. I'm so excited."

"That's good." Peter had finished only the reading part so far. That was enough. He hadn't even thought of project ideas or research.

Andrew had the DVD of the movie so Peter had seen it around a month ago. He already knew a little about the story. The project was on how the novel became a movie: Was the movie similar to the novel? Were parts left out? Were parts added? Did the characters remain consistent from the novel to the movie? Was the screenplay a good adaptation of the novel?

"I'll print this info off and bring it to school tomorrow," continued Tessa. "We have English first period."

"Is there anything you want me to do?" Peter asked, hoping she'd say no.

"That's okay. This was nothing really. But at least it gives us something to look at in class. I think we get some in-class time tomorrow to work on it. It's a start anyway. Erin said she'd do some stuff tonight too."

"Uh, okay." Peter had no idea what else to say.

Tessa waited a split second before she said, "I heard you're playing a really good team on the weekend. There's a guy named Warren Steele who's supposed to be an awesome hockey player. There was an article on you and him and another guy named Kevin Jennings from Kelowna in this free hockey magazine that my little brother picks up at the arena."

"In *Hockey Now*? Peter asked, stunned. He hadn't seen that article.

"Yup, that's the magazine," said Tessa. "I think it just came out tonight. My brother said the guy was just putting them in the box this afternoon."

"Oh," said Peter.

"Hey, when's your next home game?"

"Next Wednesday," replied Peter.

"Cool. Well, see you at school tomorrow."

"Yeah, see you." Peter hung up the phone and sat still for a few seconds, thinking about his conversation with Tessa. He was surprised she had called him, but even more than that he was baffled that another article had been written about him. He had to phone home.

Susie answered after the third ring. "Hey, Susie," said Peter.

"Oh, hi," replied Susie. Her voice lacked enthusiasm.

"What's the matter?" he asked softly. He decided not to tell Susie about Tessa.

"Karen's baby is real sick," said Susie. "They had to go to Yellowknife."

"What's wrong?"

"No one knows yet. I guess they have to run some sort of tests."

"It's good she got to Yellowknife. They have a big hospital there." He waited a second before he said, "Did you read the *Edmonton Sun* article?"

"Peter, my friend's baby is sick. Anyway, the whole thing was about that other family. It's as if they're your family instead of us, and that Christine is your sister instead of me. I don't have time for this. I have more important things to think about than you!"

12

Olds Fans

Peter was thankful when Friday arrived and school was over for the weekend. At least now he could concentrate on hockey and forget about his life, which was swirling like a chaotic hurricane around him. At first being in the newspaper had been cool, but now it seemed to be creating problems. All last night, he'd lain awake in his bed, staring at the ceiling, thinking about the phone call he'd had with Susie. Why was she so mad at him? He didn't write the article. And Peter certainly didn't think that the Pattersons were his real family. Why would she say something like that? And Christine was all cranky too. Peter wished the reporters would stop writing about him, then maybe all these problems would go away. In the morning, his eyes were heavy from lack of sleep.

When he'd checked his e-mail at lunch, Susie had sent a note saying that Karen's baby seemed to be doing better and that the doctors were giving the newborn antibiotics. The short note made Peter think that maybe Susie wasn't mad at him anymore.

Mr. Patterson dropped Peter off early for practice, as he had to drive Andrew to a game way on the north side of the city. Peter lugged his bag behind him as he entered the arena. He looked forward to the light skate, to get the pre-game kinks out and to hopefully wake up. He saw the *Hockey Now* stand and decided to pick up the newspaper to read before everyone else showed up.

Alone in the dressing room, Peter sat down and leaned against the wall for a second. What a week. In Tuk, life definitely moved at a slower pace. Peter often thought about snowmobiling and hunting to relax. He couldn't wait to go home for a visit.

He opened the newspaper and leafed through the pages until he found the article. Just like Tessa said, it was about Kevin Jennings, Warren Steele, and Peter. The writer said they were the best Bantam players in the West, the names to look for in the next Junior draft.

Tingles ran up and down Peter's spine. He rested against the cold concrete wall and shut his eyes. His life lately was like that rollercoaster ride at the Edmonton Mall. First he made the Bantam team, moved from Tuk, and almost went home. And now... his name was appearing all over the place. No one had even phoned him about this article. Could what the media was saying be true? Was he was headed for the NHL?

Peter jolted upright when he heard the dressing room door open and voices approach him.

"Hey, it's NWT boy," said Greg. Greg shifted his gaze from Peter's face to the *Hockey Now* newspaper. "Figures. You're reading about yourself."

Peter quickly folded the newspaper and shoved it under the bench. He unzipped his bag. Tanner sat down beside Peter and whispered, "Don't listen to him. He's always a jerk when his dad is home."

"I didn't even know they'd written anything," muttered Peter.

"Greg thinks he should be in the paper." Tanner rolled up a ball of tape and threw it at Greg. "He's thought that since Tyke hockey."

Greg dodged the tape, picked it up, and whipped it back at Tanner. "I'll get you good." Tanner obviously knew how to lighten Greg's moods.

"No, you won't." Tanner jumped to catch the tape. Then he did a jump shot and sunk it in the garbage can. "I can't wait to play this weekend." He sat on the bench. "Once I score a hat trick, they'll talk about me!"

"I'm scoring the hat trick!" Greg shouted.

"Who's scoring a hat trick?" Matt asked loudly as he entered the dressing room.

Peter continued to quietly dress for the practice. But his hands were shaking as he fastened his shin pads. Greg's constant comments bugged Peter more than he liked to admit.

"Tanner or I," said Greg.

"Yeah, right," said Peter, under his breath.

"I heard that some scouts might show up, and some agents too," said Matt. "They want to see Warren Steele. I've played against him since Novice, and I know he's not that good. He's just big."

"Those crazy country fans in Olds love him," said Tanner. "He's like their Wayne Gretzky. Man, they love their Bantam hockey in that town. You touch their Warren Steele and they scream. He scores they scream. Remember when we played them last year?"

Matt nodded. "He hit me so hard I crumbled like a tin can being squashed, and they all cheered. I thought the roof would blow off the arena, they were so loud."

"They'll probably sic him on Peter," said Greg with a nasty grin.

Peter looked up and stared Greg in the eyes. "I'll be ready."

After practice, Coach wanted to talk to everyone. "This will be a tough game," he said. "We have to keep our cool. The Olds fans will be out to make us lose. We have to stay calm and play our own game."

Peter glanced at all the guys then back to Coach.

Everyone was talking about the fans. Obviously, they all knew something Peter didn't.

* * *

Olds was approximately two hours from Sherwood Park. Peter was supposed to be at the arena an hour and a half early. In his bedroom after lunch, he got dressed and surprisingly managed to tie his tie perfectly. Before he left his room, he sat on the end of his bed and closed his eyes. He remembered what the sports psychologist at summer camp had taught him about creative visualization. Peter saw himself skating, passing the puck, body checking, and snapping the puck into the net. He also visualized confronting Greg, not allowing Greg's taunts and behaviour to bring him down. When Peter opened his eyes, his gaze rested on his drum. He looked at the clock and saw he had five minutes. Pulling it out, Peter drummed his fingers until it was time to go.

The entire Patterson family was going to the game, as well as Christine's friend Jemma. They were staying overnight in Red Deer so they could all go to Trevor's game on the Sunday afternoon.

In the Pattersons' van, Peter opted to sit in the back seat with Andrew. He didn't say a word for the entire drive. Mr. Patterson parked in front of the Olds arena to let Peter off. While

Peter was pulling out his equipment, Mr. Patterson got out of the van. He put his hand on Peter's shoulder and said, "Remember to play your own game. Don't get caught up in the crowd. This will be a crazy game and you're going to have to stay really focused. The fans might try to rattle you."

Peter nodded. *How bad could these fans be?* Everyone was making such a big deal about this game.

"Show everyone who you are." Mr. Patterson winked at Peter. "We're going to check in at the hotel, but we'll be back in plenty of time for the game."

Peter lifted his shoulders to inhale a huge breath before he turned and walked into the arena.

As soon as he entered the arena, he saw a group of players in shirts and ties, wearing Olds jackets. They stood by their bags.

One guy pointed to Peter and said something. Peter thought he heard the word "hotshot." The guy he was standing with glared at Peter and replied, "He's small. There's no way he'll beat Steeler."

Peter held his head high and stared at a point on the wall as he walked by them. He'd had enough of people jeering him. When Coach John tapped him on the shoulder, Peter flinched in surprise. He had been concentrating so hard that he hadn't heard anyone approach him. "Hi, Coach," he said.

"Dressing room two, Peter."

"Thanks." Peter nodded and walked down the hall.

The dressing room was eerily quiet when he entered.

"Hey, Peter," said Matt softly.

"Hey," said Peter back. A few of the guys also said "hi" but that was about it. No one threw tape, bantered, or horsed around. The team had definitely come to play focused hockey.

Peter dressed in silence. With every piece of equipment he

put on, the knots in his stomach seemed to tighten. Finally, when he was fully dressed except for his helmet, he leaned back against the concrete wall and closed his eyes. His leg jiggled up and down and, although he tried, he couldn't get it to stop. Finally, he leaned forward, placed his elbows on his thighs, and looked to the black floor.

Coach John's words from yesterday ran through his mind. Again, he visualized how he would skate and pass and shoot. How he would give-and-go. How he would cycle the puck. How he would angle, seal, and ride out his checks. How he would create picks and screens to create space. And how in his own zone he'd fight through the screen and score.

By the time Coach had said his pre-game talk and the ice was ready, Peter was fully charged for the game. The adrenalin flowed through every one of his muscles and he wanted to win.

The moment he stepped on the ice, he heard the crowd booing. The sound was deafening. It was as if they were booing in unison. He tried to ignore them, just as Coach told them to. As he skated around, the fans sitting in the first row of seats pounded the glass and yelled, "Kuiksak, go home!"

Suddenly, the entire arena erupted. "Kuiksak, go home! Kuiksak, go home! Kuiksak, go home!"

13

Steele vs. Kuiksak

The fans kept screaming Peter's name, over and over. When the warm-up was over and Coach called them over, the crowd was so loud Peter could hardly hear.

Coach motioned for the team to move in. Once everyone was squished together he said, "Don't let the fans get to you." Even though they were jammed together like bees in a hive, Coach's voice still got lost in the drone coming from the stands. Peter tried to concentrate but he kept hearing his name.

Coach had Peter on the first line again. Just as he was about to take his position at centre, Coach called to him. Peter skated back to the bench. Coach leaned in and said, "Don't let them get to you."

"I won't."

Coach patted his shoulder.

Peter skated to centre ice. The sweat was already dripping off his forehead. His stomach rumbled. He'd never been so nervous in his entire life. But he also felt something else. It almost as if he was detached from his body. His limbs seemed to move without him even trying. He wondered if this was how the old shamans in his hamlet felt when they were going on a journey. He'd seen them concentrate and focus, and then leave the earth for periods of time. They always said they could fly to the moon when they were on a journey. Maybe this was the same thing.

Matt skated beside him and said, "You can beat Steeler. Get it back if you can, then we can control the play right from the start."

Peter blew out a big rush of air and nodded in a small gesture. "Yeah," he said. When he bent over at the face-off, he stared at the puck in the referee's hand and didn't blink. He knew if he lost his concentration for even a brief milli-second he'd lose the face-off. He'd planned this face-off in his mind in the dressing room and now it was running like a commercial that got too much air time.

When the puck dropped, Peter nudged his shoulder into Warren Steele while backhanding the puck. They both batted at it, but Peter ended up the winner. The crowd booed like crazy, rattling the glass, screaming his name, telling him to, go home.

Peter moved his feet. He rushed up the ice. On defence, Dylan snapped the puck up the boards. Tanner picked it up on his wing, bounced it off the boards, and wheeled around. Once it was back on his stick, Tanner used his soft hands to stick-handle and weave forward. Without breaking his stride, he sped over the blue line.

Peter glanced over to see where Matt was. He trailed Peter by less than a stride, so Matt would have to play third-man back. Peter could hear the sound of edges digging into the ice. Someone was on his tail, back-checking. The crowd was no longer screaming Peter's name, telling him to go home. They were chanting "Steeler, Steeler."

Warren Steele was catching Peter. Three strides. Two strides. Peter dug his edges in, harder and harder. He skated toward the net. He tapped his stick on the ice. Suddenly, he was hooked from behind.

"Steeler, Steeler!" the crowd roared.

Peter swung around, trying to dodge Warren Steele. But the big player was relentless. He stuck to Peter like glue. Peter tried to get open, break the screen. The Olds defence cross-checked Peter, sending him flying back. Peter pursued, keeping his feet moving, hoping to get open.

Tanner drilled the puck around the boards in a strong effort to hit Matt on the other side. Matt picked it up but was immediately checked. Suddenly, Warren Steele took off, leaving Peter open. Peter glanced over to see the Olds player snipe the puck from Matt and slap it forward. Steele had anticipated the break through the middle. Now he had it and was flying toward Stu.

The crowd went beserk. "Steeler! Steeler!"

Peter gritted his teeth and skated forward, wanting to help the Arrows defence, who had been caught standing.

Peter had to get him.

One more length of the ice and Peter knew his legs would give out. One more length, that's all he had to skate. His thighs burned in agony as he tried to catch Warren Steele. Steele headed straight down the middle until he hit the red line. Then he went wide, as any smart player would do.

Peter saw the Arrows defence try to stop Steele, but he made a fancy move by kicking the puck with his skates to make a pass to himself. He threw Dylan off and totally undressed him. By now Peter was at full stride and there was no way he would stop. He had to angle Steele and place a seal between him and the net. He rubbed shoulders with the Olds player. Then he pushed him toward the boards with a body-check. Peter clenched his mouthpiece with his teeth and used his entire body to make the hit.

He felt the contact. He saw stars. The glass shook. The fans screamed and hammered their fists on the glass in front of him. Both Peter and Steele went down. Peter could see the loose puck in front of him. He tried to swat at it. Steele pushed on Peter's shoulder to get up, keeping Peter down longer than he wanted to be. A player from the Olds team took a shot. Stu made a save.

The whistle blew.

Peter skated to the bench. One shift, and he felt as if he'd played an entire game.

"Great shift, Peter," said Coach, smacking his back. "Get some rest and drink lots of water. I want you ready right away."

Peter sat on the bench and put his head between his knees, breathing deeply. He had been sitting for only thirty seconds or so when he heard his name.

"Peter, you ready?" Coach asked from his standing position on the bench.

"Yup." He swigged some water.

"I want you in for Greg." Coach leaned over. "I'm trying to throw them off by getting you out so quickly. They'll try to keep Steele on you. You have to get open immediately before he has time to get on the ice."

Peter gave a few short nods. When he tried to get in closer to the boards so he could jump over, Tanner wouldn't move to let him in.

"Tanner," said Peter, "move over. I'm on next."

"Greg!" Coach John waved like crazy for Greg to come off. Greg glanced at the bench, but when the play started toward him, he made a decision not to come off.

"Tanner, move!" Peter still had to swing his legs to get over.

"Peter, be ready," said Coach, almost in a panic. "You're on as soon as he's off."

Peter pushed Tanner so he could get close to the boards.

Coach wanted him ready and Tanner was stopping him from doing that. Tanner pushed Peter back.

"Tanner, I don't want to see that. I want you to sit the next shift!" Coach sounded angry.

"What?" Tanner slammed his stick.

"You slam your stick again and I'll send you to the dressing room. I don't care how good you are. Now, move over for Peter!" Coach cupped his hands around his mouth. "Greg!"

Tanner slumped and sat down. The rest of the bench fell silent. Tanner scowled at Peter.

When Greg skated to the bench he asked, "Why am I off?"

Peter hopped over the boards.

The Arrows defence had the puck and, when he saw Peter, he rimmed it hard around the boards. In a stroke of luck, the puck took a bounce and skipped by the Olds defence on the blue line. Peter hadn't crossed the blue line yet so, when the puck came out, he swooped toward it, picked it up, and pivoted. He powered his first two strides. Out of the corner of his eye he could see the other Olds defence rushing back, skating on an angle, obviously trying to push Peter into the corner. Peter increased his speed.

He had to get close.

He had to take a shot.

He heard his name. Matt was behind him. Closer to the net, Peter wound up for a slapshot. But instead of shooting he drop-passed the puck behind him. At a full skate, Matt one-timed the puck. The combined power of his speed and his shot sent the puck flying. It zinged over the goalie's shoulder and into the top corner.

Matt started running on his skates in a victory dance. Peter rushed over.

"You nailed it!" said Peter in excitement.

"Great pass!" Matt hugged Peter. Then the rest of the line jumped on them.

Matt skated down the line of guys on the Arrows bench, high-fiving everyone. He said, "Come on, let's keep the momentum going!"

"Great work, guys," said Coach John. "Peter, that was an unselfish play. Good for you. That's called teamwork. We're only up by one though. Let's take it to them and get another one. Peter and Matt, you won't be sitting long, so get ready."

Peter heard a few grumblings down the bench, especially from guys who weren't seeing much ice time, but he tried to ignore it. After all, he wasn't the only one being put out every other shift. Matt was playing as much as Peter. And it wasn't as if it was their fault. Coach was the one making all the line-change decisions.

"No one likes you," Greg whispered to Peter as they sat on the bench.

"I don't care," retorted Peter. He lifted his cage and slugged back some water. After he snapped the spout down on his water battle, he said, "Anyway, you're wrong, Matt does."

* * *

Midway through the third period, Peter knew he was having the game of his life. Never had he played this hard for this long. Coach kept putting him out, and Peter kept rising to play. About halfway through the second period, the burning in his legs had been so painful he thought he was going to seize up. He had come off that shift breathing so forcefully he thought his lungs would collapse from lack of air. He was about to tell Coach he needed a break when he heard his name. Over the boards he went.

That had been his turn-around shift. He'd swerved around

Warren Steele to fire a shot right through the five-hole, and his adrenalin snapped him into overdrive.

Now he was ready, every shift, to play hard hockey. On the bench, Peter rested his chin on his stick and glanced at the scoreboard. There was just ten minutes left in the game. The Arrows were up 4–3. Peter had scored two goals and assisted on two. Warren Steele had scored two goals for Olds as well. The Arrows had to play good defence to hold off the Olds team.

The fans were really screaming now. For Peter, the noise had become like really loud rock music in the dressing room.

As the clock ticked, the Arrows held their lead. Finally, the game was at the one-minute mark. The Olds goalie skated toward the net. Peter was on the ice with Matt, Tanner, and two Arrows defence. Olds had control and were cycling the puck like crazy. From winger to defence to winger then back to defence, who sent it over to the other defence. The fans were going bananas.

"Shoot," they screamed. "Someone shoot!"

Now Warren Steele had the puck. He wound up for a shot. Peter reacted without thinking and skated in front of Steele! When he saw Steele's stick connect, Peter quickly shut his eyes.

The puck struck his thigh. His eyes watered from the burning sensation. Through his hazy view, Peter could see that the puck had bounced out past the blue line. Still dazed, he raced toward it, wound up, and shot it as hard as he could. The puck against his stick made a cracking noise. Someone checked him from behind the second the puck left his stick. He lost his balance and crashed to the ice.

Before he had time to get up, he felt the dog-pile.

Peter had scored on an empty net.

14

Interested Agent

The red mark on Peter's thigh was as big as a baseball.

"Whoa, that is going to be one ugly bruise," said Matt. Peter sat between Matt and Dylan.

Peter nursed his leg with an ice pack. None of the guys had said too much to Peter after the game. He still felt the hostility that had been apparent on the bench. Greg had always been nasty to Peter, and Peter thought it was because his dad always yelled at him, but now it seemed as if Tanner was going to follow him. But the Arrows were a team and they had won. Everyone should be happy.

Dylan grimaced as he looked at Peter icing his leg. "Steele has such a hard shot. I can't believe you went in front of it."

From his seat three players down, Stu leaned forward and said, "Yeah, even I cringe when the guy shoots. And I've got tons of equipment on."

Peter lifted the ice pack to take a look. It was all red and there was no doubt it was going to be one big bruise. He put the ice pack on the bench, knowing he had to get dressed. Most of the guys were already showered and ready to go.

"I heard Olds is in the Kelowna tournament as well," said Matt. "That Kevin Jennings will be there too. I'd like to see him up against Warren Steele."

"That's going to be a hard tournament," said Dylan, wanting to be part of the conversation.

"I went to camp with that guy," said Peter. His memories of Kevin were not great. Kevin had actually been quite nasty to Peter.

"Is he as good as everyone says?" Matt tossed his wet hair as he stood. He put on his jacket in preparation to leave.

"He's good," replied Peter.

"That's it?" Matt looked at Peter funny. "I've heard he's awesome."

"I, uh, scored more goals than him," replied Peter.

From the distance, Peter heard Greg say to Tanner. "Told you NWT boy thought he was good. What a jerk."

"Why don't you just be quiet?" said Peter. "You're always mouthing off for no reason."

Tanner stood and yanked his bag over to the door with Greg on his heels. Both boys glared at Peter.

Matt looked over his shoulder at Greg and Tanner and said, "I'll meet you guys in the lobby, okay? Don't leave without me."

"We won't leave without *you*," said Tanner. "You're not high on yourself."

"Wait for me," said Dylan to Tanner and Greg. "I'm coming now too." He quickly put on his jacket, avoiding eye contact with Peter.

Peter watched Dylan trail Tanner and Greg out of the dressing room. Why was he ditching Peter too? Peter decided his best bet was to ignore them all for now. He'd had just about enough.

When the door shut, Matt turned to Peter and said, "There

were agents here tonight, you know. Dan Andrews was one of them. I'd do anything to get signed with him. He's one of the best."

"I don't know too much about agents," muttered Peter. He still felt stung by the other guys. And angry too.

"My dad says it's a good thing for me to get one now, because they can help my career."

Peter didn't reply.

"Well, see you," said Matt. He held up a thumb. "Monday at practice, I'll tell you who my agent is."

One by one, the guys filed out of the dressing room, leaving Peter by himself. The silence in the room was almost as deafening as the crowd had been. It was weird. He hardly had any quiet time anymore, but now that he had a few minutes to himself he couldn't let his mind relax. He'd been on a high and now he was on a low. How could that happen so fast? Greg had been upset with his quote in the *Gazette.* Then Susie got mad at him for the article in the *Edmonton Sun.* And now, when he'd been honest about Kevin Jennings, the guys all walked out on him. Even Dylan. What was with that?

Peter shook his head. The Arrows had won, Peter had played the best game of his life, but he felt lousy inside. He zipped up his bag and slipped on his coat.

"What a great game!" said Mr. Patterson when Peter walked into the arena lobby. "You were unbelievable, Peter. I think that's the best game I've seen you play. You didn't back down."

"Thanks," replied Peter, trying to smile.

"What's the matter?"

"Nothing." Peter looked to the ground. "I'm tired."

"How's your leg? You took a nasty puck in the thigh."

Peter lifted his head and cocked a half-smile at Mr. Patterson. "Bruised. But I'm okay."

"Your coach wants to talk to you," said Mr. Patterson.

"Why?" Peter furrowed his eyebrows. He didn't want to talk to anyone. All he wanted to do was go directly to the hotel to watch television in the room he was sharing with Andrew. It was adjoined to the Pattersons' room by a door. Christine was bunking with her parents.

Mr. Patterson grinned from ear to ear. "He's got some great news for you."

When Peter and Mr. Patterson approached Coach, he was standing with another man who was dressed in a suit and tie, looking important.

"Peter," said Coach John. "I'd like you to meet Dan Andrews. He's Rick Murdock's agent."

Confused, Peter shook the man's hand. Rick Murdock won Rookie of the Year in the NHL last year. "Hi," mumbled Peter.

"He'd like to talk to you and your family about possible representation."

"Uh, my dad lives in the Northwest Territories."

"We were thinking that since your billet, Mr. Patterson, has been through this with his son Trevor, he might be the person you could have help you." Coach John smiled at Peter. "What do you think?"

"Okay," said Peter. His father should be all right with this. After all, he didn't really know a lot about hockey and Mr. Patterson did.

Dan Andrews smiled at Peter. "I know it's late and you're probably tired, but I heard you're staying in Red Deer so you can watch a Junior game tomorrow. Why don't we meet for breakfast in the morning?"

Peter looked to Mr. Patterson, who would be doing the driving, for affirmation. Mr. Patterson put his hand on Peter's shoulder. Then he looked to Dan Andrews and said, "Perfect.

Name a restaurant and time and we'll be there."

* * *

That night in the hotel, Peter was in a funny mood. He couldn't explain it but he felt good, bad, and sad, all at the same time. He wondered if some of the other guys had talked about him on the drive home.

Peter lay under the crisp hotel sheets, watching a horror movie with Andrew. Andrew talked non-stop through the movie, hiding and screaming every time a scary part came on. A few times, Peter wanted to tell him to be quiet and stop squirming, but he let the younger boy natter on about nothing.

Peter knew he should phone home to tell his dad about the game and the agent, but he was tired and his leg was sore. He knew Andrew would listen to his side of the conversation. He didn't want anyone from the Patterson family to know that Susie might be mad at him. He told himself that it would be better to phone tomorrow after the meeting because then he would have more information. What would his dad say about all of this? What would his dad say about him making decisions without talking to him? He should phone home.

Before the movie ended, Peter fell asleep.

15

Peter's Dad

The next morning, Peter's bruise covered the front of his thigh. Andrew took one look at it and made a big scene.

"It's just a bruise," said Peter.

"I know, but it's so-oo big and gross looking."

"I don't have to play today, so it will be okay by Monday."

"I can't wait to go to Trevor's game tonight." Andrew hopped up and down on the hotel bed. "We get to go down to the dressing room."

There was a knock on the adjoining door. "Peter," said Mr. Patterson from the other side, "we'll leave in fifteen minutes."

"Where are you going?" Andrew was still jumping on the bed.

"A meeting."

Andrew stopped jumping and looked at Peter, wide-eyed. "Did you get signed to a Junior team already?"

"Not quite. It's a meeting with an agent."

"Wow! I knew you were going to be famous one day."

Peter tried to smile. This fame thing came with lots of headaches.

At the restaurant, after Peter ordered his bacon and eggs and orange juice, he sat quietly, not sure how to act. Mr. Patterson was deep in conversation with Dan Andrews.

"I heard the team has money problems," said Mr. Patterson.

Dan Andrews shook his head. "It's not good."

"Do you think they'll fold?"

"Not sure. They're not getting the bodies out to games."

Peter had no idea what they were talking about. He fidgeted. He crossed his hands then uncrossed them. He glanced around the restaurant, staring at the pictures on the walls. Suddenly, he heard his name. He turned his gaze back to the table. Both men were staring at him. He hadn't heard what they'd said. "What was that?" he blurted out. His face flushed.

"I said, you played a heck of a game last night, Peter," said Dan Andrews.

"Thanks." Peter was saved from saying anything else by the waitress arriving with their breakfast.

"Dan, here, can help further your career, Peter," said Mr. Patterson after the waitress had left. "He figures you might be drafted next spring."

"Drafted?" Peter almost choked on his first bite of his toast. "I'm only first-year Bantam."

"And right now, I'd say you're the top Bantam in the country." Dan Andrews casually dunked his toast in his eggs. He took a bite before he said, "That's incredible for your age. There hasn't been a Bantam like you since Sidney Crosby. And before that, Wayne Gretzky."

Peter quickly glanced at Mr. Patterson. *Is this true?*

Mr. Patterson smiled, trying to put Peter at ease. "You have a future in hockey, Peter, if you want it."

"Peter," said Dan leaning forward, "I take few players on. You're the only one from your team I want. And the only first-year

Bantam. Last night I went to see Warren Steele, but he doesn't compare to you. I think you have a future."

"What about Matt?" Peter asked as he stared at Dan Andrews.

"Matt is a good player. But as I said, I rarely take on first-year Bantams. You're an exception. Someone else will pick him up."

Peter felt his eggs spinning donuts in his stomach. Wait until Matt heard Peter was with Dan Andrews. For some reason, he dreaded Matt finding out.

Mr. Patterson leaned forward and clasped his hands together. "Peter, we're here to talk about you today. No one else. This is your career we're talking about. You need to decide if you want a career in hockey."

"I do want a career in hockey only…" Peter lowered his head, unable to finish his sentence. He wished he could talk to his dad, but he was worried that would make him look like he didn't care. Back in Tuk, his biggest decision had been whether he wanted to go to school or not, or whether he wanted to hunt or harpoon fish. This could be the chance of a lifetime and he didn't know what to do. The eggs were now longer spinning in his stomach. They were sitting in the bottom like heavy stones.

"Only what, Peter?" Mr. Patterson asked gently, breaking Peter out of his silent spell.

Peter looked from Mr. Patterson to Dan, then back to Mr. Patterson. "I, uh, want a career in hockey." He said the words with as much conviction as he could muster.

Mr. Patterson patted his shoulder. "You won't be sorry, Peter. This is a good move."

Then Dan smiled and said, "Welcome aboard, Peter. We do have some paperwork to fill out."

Peter nodded. "Should we talk to my dad?"

Mr. Patterson took his cell phone out of his jacket pocket. "Why don't you call him?"

Peter punched in the number but got the answering machine. "Hi, Dad. It's Peter. Call me right away, okay? On Mr. Patterson's cell phone." He paused, but just for a split second. Then he said quietly, "We won last night. I scored two goals."

When Peter handed the cell phone back to Mr. Patterson, Dan Andrews said, "I'd like to talk to your father as well. If we come to an agreement, I'll be in touch to send the papers to both of you." He looked Peter in the eyes. "You have nothing to worry about. I'll take good care of you."

* * *

Peter didn't hear from his dad until later that evening, just before the Red Deer Junior game was to start. When Mr. Patterson handed Peter the phone, Peter walked to a corner so he could have a private conversation.

"Hey," said Mr. Kuiksak, "so you got another two goals. Good for you."

Peter didn't really want to make small talk with his dad, because he knew he had to talk to him about the agent.

"Listen, Dad," said Peter slowly, trying to figure out how to handle this situation, "There's an agent interested in me. His name is Dan Andrews and Mr. Patterson says he's one of the best. We met for breakfast this morning. Mr. Patterson thinks I should sign with him."

There was a silence on the other end of the phone. Then his father said, "Mr. Patterson?"

"Yeah. He knows his stuff, Dad."

"You don't think I can handle this for you?" His dad's voice was quiet.

"It's not that."

Silence.

"Dad, Mr. Patterson has been through this before. He knows what to do and he knows who's good. Dan Andrews wants to talk to you too."

There was more silence on the other end of the phone. "It sounds as if you don't need me to talk to anyone, Peter. But then I guess it's your hockey. Your life. Do what you think is best."

"Did you want to talk to Mr. Patterson now? I could get him for you."

"No. Call me later. Tell that agent to call me too. I'm your father, you know."

16

Trevor's Advice

Peter tried to forget his conversation with his dad and concentrate on the Junior game. Andrew jumped around, eating popcorn and spilling it everywhere. Peter wished he could enjoy Andrew's enthusiasm.

Life in Tuk had been so much easier. He spent his days hunting and fishing and hanging out with friends. He didn't have to think about making decisions, or what to say to reporters or agents. He didn't have to worry about kids wanting to be his friend just because he was in the newspaper. Is that the only reason Tessa and Erin wanted to work with him on a project, and why Dylan wanted to be his friend? He didn't want anyone disliking him because he was garnering attention. And he didn't have to listen to fans who cheered for him to go home.

Andrew stood up so fast he knocked half the popcorn out of his bag and onto Peter's lap. "Go, Trevor!" Andrew screamed.

Trevor Patterson had a breakaway and was heading toward the net. He skillfully deked the goalie and roofed the puck. Andrew hopped up and down. Then he slapped Christine on the back. "Trevor scored!"

She clapped happily along with the rest of the crowd. Peter studied Trevor as he headed to his bench. He was obviously the best person on his team. From the pictures and trophies in the Pattersons' house, he had also been the best in Sherwood Park. How did he handle everything? What was his secret?

Peter watched the rest of the game with a different eye. Red Deer won 4–0 and Trevor scored three of the four goals. Immediately following the game, Andrew tugged on Peter's jacket. "Come on," he said. "We can go downstairs. My dad will take us."

Andrew ran ahead, but Peter followed behind Mr. Patterson.

"What did you think of the game?" asked Mr. Patterson.

"It was good. Trevor played great," replied Peter.

"He's had his ups and downs along the way," said Mr. Patterson. "But now it seems to be coming together."

Peter frowned.

"Ups and downs? Christine said Trevor was always good."

"Well, other kids were jealous. Girls phoned him all the time. It was more of that kind of stuff. And, Mrs. Patterson and I will admit, he thought a little too much of himself at times." Mr. Patterson winked at Peter. "We put him in his place. Or should I say, Christine did."

"I bet," said Peter.

Mr. Patterson laughed.

They took the last step and were in the underbelly of the arena. Peter gazed around. He loved everything about an arena, especially that distinct smell. Christine called it the sweaty-gear smell. Peter inhaled. It smelled like home to him, just like the ocean water in Tuk smelled like home.

"This way," said Mr. Patterson. They walked under the stands. The walls were covered with pictures of teams and players from years gone by. *That would be something, to have your picture in an arena,* thought Peter.

Mr. Patterson put his hand on Peter's shoulder. "Feel free to talk to Trevor. He may help answer some of your questions."

* * *

Peter stared at everything in the dressing room, from the lockers where the players put their stuff, to the mound of bags, to the physio room. A medical trainer ripped tape from one player's legs. So this was Junior hockey. Was this Peter's next step?

When the good players finished playing Junior, they could move up to play in the NHL. Mr. Patterson had explained to Peter that some kids went on to college scholarships, but Trevor had decided to play Junior. His best friend was playing at Maine University in the States. Did these guys have problems with parents and teammates too?

"Trevor!" Andrew ran toward his brother and hugged him around the waist. Trevor was dressed but his shirt was still unbuttoned. *The guy is ripped,* thought Peter.

"Hey, squirt." Trevor tousled Andrew's hair. Then he glanced over at Peter. "You had quite a game last night."

Peter nodded.

"He wants to get the shirt he bought signed for his family," said Andrew.

"Sure," said Trevor.

Peter handed him the T-shirt without saying anything. This one he was giving to his brother for his birthday. Trevor took the shirt, signed it with the marker Peter brought, then passed them both to the guy beside him. As Trevor buttoned up his own shirt he said, "You better watch how it's done, Peter. You'll be signing autographs before you know it."

"He already did. For my friends."

Trevor laughed and put Andrew in a headlock.

"Are you ripping your friends off again?"

"I made five bucks." Andrew squirmed out of the headlock. Are you coming for dinner with us?"

"You bet."

Peter sat next to Trevor at dinner. Mr. Patterson sat on his other side. Just before the meal arrived, Mr. and Mrs. Patterson were in a conversation with Christine, and Andrew had headed off to the bathroom. This left Peter with Trevor.

Trevor turned and asked, "How's everything?"

"Okay," he mumbled.

"You played amazing last night."

"Thanks."

"You should be happier than that."

Peter shrugged. "Being in the media makes everything kind of weird."

Trevor nodded knowingly. "Yeah. It's neat when it happens, then it ends up being a lot of pressure."

Peter stared down at the yellow table cloth. That was true, for sure.

Trevor continued talking. "I read this article on Sidney Crosby, and he said he focuses on meeting his own expectations, not the ones other people set for him. I'm trying to do that. You should too."

"Is it hard to do that?" Peter spun his glass of water around in circles.

"Yeah. Big-time hard. Do you know there are girls who wait outside for us after our games? They don't know us, but they wait for us. My girlfriend gets so ticked at them. And guys and even coaches get mad if you're not scoring all the time. And then other guys get jealous if you *are* scoring. It's like you're expected to score and win the game for the team, but not score so you're not better than everyone. And if you have a bad game the media will write how you're in a slump. And if you're good they write good things. I think the thing is to ignore it and just play hockey."

"Okay." That was a lot of info for Peter to absorb. The only thing he really understood was how to just play hockey.

Trevor paused. "I read your article in the *Gazette*."

"I blew that one," said Peter.

"Next time, make sure you give your team credit too. Always say something good about them. And don't ever let your ego take control, or you'll say negative things. That gets you in big-time trouble. I did that in high school."

Peter sipped his water before he asked, "What happened?"

"I thought I was way too cool. Then I lost respect for myself. I hated looking in the mirror because I knew I wasn't a good role model. That's a horrible feeling."

"At first I liked the write-ups," said Peter, "but now they seem to be causing problems."

"Fame does weird things to people. People get jealous and stuff. I think this might be harder for you."

"Because I'm from the North."

"More because you're playing with guys you haven't played with before. In Bantam, I played with guys I had always played with. You've come from somewhere else and never played with any of those guys. My dad told me how hard it is on you. Who knows, maybe you took a position away from one of their friends." Trevor snatched a bread roll from the basket in the middle of the table.

"My sister's kind of mad at me too," said Peter. "And Christine."

Trevor rolled his eyes. "Sisters keep you in your place."

Peter bit into his own bread roll and swallowed before he said. "Did you hear the fans booing me?"

Trevor smiled. "That's okay. When they get involved, it's

good, because it keeps the game alive. We need fans." Trevor ripped his bread in half and buttered it.

"I thought they were booing at me because I was from the North."

"Nah." Trevor grinned. "You score goals. Fans either like you or hate you. They hated you in Olds because you're not from there. Road trips are always harder. If you want to be in the NHL one day, you better get used to that."

"I do want to be in the NHL," said Peter quietly.

"Then don't get too caught up in all this stuff. It'll wreck your hockey if you do."

17

More Ups and Downs

Even though it was late when they arrived back in Edmonton, Peter went to his room and picked up the phone. He punched in the numbers three times before he finally let the phone ring.

"Hey, Dad," said Peter.

"Pete. What's up?"

"Nothing. I just wanted to phone and see how Karen was doing with her baby."

"I'll get Susie for you."

"Dad, before you go," Peter paused for a split second, "I want you to help me with all of this, okay?"

"I don't know that much."

"You know *me* better than anyone. Would you talk to Mr. Patterson for me? Please."

"You sure you want me to?"

"Yeah, I'm sure."

"Okay, Peter. You must be doing real good."

"When are you going to come down and watch a game?" Peter looked longingly at his Inuit drum in the open closet. He missed his dad.

"Soon. I don't think Susie is going to come, though. She's too scared to get on a plane. When I come, I want to meet this Andrews guy."

"I'm sure we can set that up if he's not too busy."

"Okay. And I'll talk to Mr. Patterson about all of this, but not tonight. I'm too tired."

"I know. Maybe tomorrow."

"I'll get Susie for you."

When Susie came on the phone Peter immediately said, "Hi, Susie. How's Karen?"

"The baby's doing lots better. I think they're coming home tomorrow."

"That's good. Say hi to her for me. I've got something for her from a game I went to yesterday. I'll send it right away. How's Lisa?"

"She's still awake. I can't get her to bed at night. Dad spoils her just like he used to do with you."

Peter laughed. "Me? What about you?"

"Yeah, right, Mr. Hockey Star."

Peter paused then quietly said, "Are you, uh, still mad at me?"

"Sort of."

"Things got a bit out of control." Peter played with the telephone cord.

"Just because you're getting famous doesn't mean you can forget about us or think we don't know anything."

"I haven't forgotten about you. I've been phoning more now than ever."

"You made Dad upset."

"Everything's okay now. Anyway, being in the newspaper and stuff isn't as great as it seems."

"Come on. It must be. You're lying to make me not mad at you anymore."

"No, I'm serious. It just makes everyone act strange."

"Jason and Mike want to know about the girls that are after you."

Peter smiled to himself. Why not make *this* work in his favour? "You've got to tell them — two of the hottest girls in the school asked me to be a partner for a project."

Susie burst out laughing. "They asked *you*? You're not even all that smart."

"Be quiet. Just tell them for me. Two girls, not just one."

* * *

On Monday morning, Peter was standing by his locker when he heard someone say, "Hey, Peter."

He turned to see Tessa. She held her books out in front of her. Her long red hair was pulled back in a ponytail and she wore a big Okanagan Hockey School sweatshirt. Peter had seen it somewhere before.

"Hi," he said.

"I heard you played amazing on the weekend."

"The whole team did." He shut his locker with his foot, then snapped the lock shut. Peter wondered who she'd been talking too.

"Your team is really good. I've heard you're the best Bantam team in the country."

"We have Stu and that helps. I was lucky to be on a line with Matt," said Peter walking toward the classroom. He glanced at Tessa out of the corner of his eye. Her face went as red as her hair when Peter mentioned Matt's name.

"I'm coming to your game on Wednesday," she said. She rearranged her books on her hip. "Matt invited me. I think Erin might come too." She gave him a quirky smile.

That's where Peter had seen the sweatshirt before. *On Matt.* Matt had gone to that hockey school last summer. Tessa must have been talking to him yesterday. Peter had no idea how to answer her, so he just nodded. He thought about Susie telling Mike and Jason about Tessa and Erin. Peter smiled inside. Being far away had its advantages. They didn't have to know Tessa actually liked Matt.

"He's a bit bummed from the weekend," continued Tessa. "He's happy you won, but I guess none of the important people who watched the game phoned him. I understand a little about how he feels. We had some people from the national team come watch my volleyball team play, and I was hoping they'd pick me for a junior camp."

"They didn't?" Peter was totally at a loss for words, and didn't really want to talk about this anymore.

"Nah. Oh, well. Hey, listen, I've got lots of information for our project," she said as they entered the classroom.

Peter breathed a sigh of relief. He just wanted to sit down. "I didn't have a lot of time on the weekend to do too much," he replied, "but I'll do some work tonight after practice."

"Perfect," she said. "We're going to do great on this project. I love the book. And the movie was awesome too, so it shouldn't be too hard."

"I'm only halfway through the book," admitted Peter. "But I've seen the movie."

Tessa's eyes lit up in excitement. "I think we should do a diorama like the movie set. I went to the author's website and there was a contact e-mail. So Erin and I wrote up a bunch of questions and e-mailed him. Wouldn't it be neat if he e-mailed back?" She smiled. "Thanks for working with us, Peter. At first I didn't know if this would work, but I wanted to help you out 'cause you're new and all."

"Uh, thanks."

Peter smiled at Tessa as if a weight had been lifted off his back. Minute by minute things changed. He was glad to know she picked him because he was new, and not because he was a face in the newspaper.

18

Actions Speak Louder Than Words

Peter, do you have the answer to question twenty-two?" The teacher stood at the front of the room.

"Um, did you say twenty-two?" Peter looked down at his textbook. How did they get to question twenty-two already?

"Pay attention, Peter." The teacher's voice was sharp. Peter flipped to the next page to try to find out where they were. He'd been thinking about how to tell Matt about Dan Andrews, and had missed ten questions.

When the lunch bell rang, Peter decided he would go directly to the computer room instead of the lunch room. He shoved his books in his locker, grabbed his lunch, and hurriedly shut the door.

"Hey, Peter," said Dylan, sneaking up on him. "I'll sit with you at lunch."

"I have to e-mail my sister, so I'm going to the library," said Peter.

"Too bad you didn't come for dinner with us on Saturday after the game," said Dylan.

"Where'd you guys go?"

"Some place on the way home. They had these great arcade games. Tanner and I beat Greg and Stu at everything."

"Cool."

"Hey, listen, you want to do something this weekend?"

"Maybe."

"You sure you don't want to go to the cafeteria?" Dylan asked again. "Matt said he'd save us a spot."

"Nah, that's okay. I'll see you at practice tonight though."

* * *

Peter carried his hockey bag down the arena lobby and toward dressing room one. The Arrows had early practice today, so Mrs. Patterson had picked up Peter from school and dropped him off early.

Pushing open the door, he saw Matt. Peter quickly looked around the dressing room. He hoped someone else was early too, so he wouldn't have to be alone with Matt asking him a million questions.

"What's up, Peter?"

"Not much." Peter plunked down on the bench.

"I heard the Red Deer Juniors won on Saturday night. Must have been a good game to watch." Matt was engrossed in taping his stick.

"It was," replied Peter. He opened up the plastic container to see what snack Mrs. Patterson had made for him. There were three banana chocolate chip muffins. She also packed two cheese strings. "Trevor Patterson scored a hat trick." Peter took a bite out of one of the muffins.

"Yeah, I read that in the newspaper," said Matt. "He's doing awesome. I heard they're looking at him for the World Junior Team that plays at Christmas. That tournament is in Vancouver this year. My dad's trying to get tickets." Matt wound black tape around the top of his stick to make a knob.

"That would be such a great tournament to play in. It's like the best Juniors from all over the world." Peter popped a straw in a juice box.

"The year Canada played Russia in the final game," said Matt, "it was such a good game. One day, I want to be on that team."

Peter unzipped his bag and pulled out his thermal underwear. It was too early to get dressed, so Peter sat back to finish his snack.

The room became silent. Matt finished taping his stick. Peter finished his first muffin.

"I heard you have an agent," said Matt, leaning his stick against the wall.

Peter jerked his head up. "Who, did, uh, you hear that from?"

Matt laughed and shook his head at Peter. "You billet with Christine Patterson. It was all over school today."

This was not the reaction Peter had expected. He was sure Matt was going to be angry with him, like Tanner and Greg had been on Saturday night.

"Way to go," he said. "My turn will come if I keep playing hard."

"You're not mad," said Peter in surprise.

"Nah. Just disappointed. But you know, I read this article on Sidney Crosby, and he says it's important to meet your own expectations. I'm trying to do that."

"Trevor Patterson told me that too," said Peter. "You guys

must have read the same magazine."

"Yeah, probably. I try to read about players who seem to have it together." Matt stood and whipped his sweatshirt over his head. It was the same one Tessa had been wearing at school.

Peter grinned. "Wasn't Tessa wearing that shirt this morning?"

"It stinks like flowers." Matt wrinkled his nose. "I never should have let her wear it."

"You want a muffin?" Peter offered.

"I was wondering when you were going to give me one."

Peter glanced quickly at Matt. No wonder he was named captain, he had the good leadership skills. Peter knew he could learn a lot from Matt.

Peter hesitated before he asked, "How do you think the other guys will react to me getting an agent?" He honestly wanted Matt's opinion.

Matt flipped his hair out of his eyes. "Greg will act like a jerk, as usual. He's been like that since Tyke hockey. Every year he hates someone. One year it was me. Right now his dad is comparing him to you all the time, and that's why he hates you. But he's okay. He doesn't mean half of what he says. There's no point in fighting back. And Tanner will be okay too. He'll go with Greg for a little. He does that because he's known him for so many years. But he's a team player. As for the rest of the guys, welcome to Bantam hockey. Every year kids in Bantam get agents."

"You'll get an agent too," said Peter.

"My dad and I talked on the way home," replied Matt, gazing down at the muffin in his hand. "And I actually don't care as much about getting an agent as I do about getting a college scholarship." Matt quickly peeled the paper off the muffin, then shoved the entire muffin into his mouth.

"You're lucky," said Peter. "You're smart in school. Most kids where I'm from don't go past grade nine."

Through a mouth full of muffin, Matt said, "You'll get a good mark on your English project. Tessa's smarter than me." He grinned. "You should go after Erin."

Peter shook his head. "I don't think so."

"She likes you."

"Do you think she'd like me if I wasn't a hockey player?"

"But you are. So why even ask that question?"

"Gross. You just spit muffin on me." Peter didn't want to talk about Erin any more, even though the thought of her liking him made him happy.

"Good, "said Matt, wiping his mouth. "We've got to toughen up if we're going to kick some serious butt in Kelowna."

As Peter held up his hand for a high-five, Tanner shoved the door open with his foot to enter the dressing room. "Who's going to kick butt in Kelowna?" He asked.

"The Arrows," yelled Matt. "Who else?"

"I brought some new tunes." Greg barrelled through the door waving some CDs, Dylan on his heels. Greg stopped when he saw Peter. "Hey, NWT boy, I heard you're a big shot with an agent now."

"You're just jealous," said Matt.

Peter glanced at Matt and whispered, "I can handle this," he whispered.

Then Peter grinned and threw a wad of tape at Greg. "So? Who cares? The Arrows still have to kick butt in Kelowna."

"Arrows, Arrows," yelled Matt.

Instantly, the rest of the guys in the dressing room joined in Matt's chant, including Peter.